Astrid V.J.

First edition December 2020
Editing by Joy Sephton
Cover design by Emily's World of Design

ISBN 978-91-985519-7-6 (paperback)
ISBN 978-91-985519-8-3 (ebook)
ISBN 978-91-985519-9-0 (audiobook)

Published by New Wings Press
Oluff Nilssonsväg 10, Partille, Sweden

This is a work of fiction. It is the combined product of the collective subconscious as transmitted by the students of human potential and transformation, including but not limited to, Viktor Frankl, Mary Morrissey, Henry David Thoreau, the Greek Philosophers and Napoleon Hill and the imagination of the author. Any similarities to the real world are either a product of the human experience—we are humans with shared human emotions, experiences and responses—or entirely coincidental. Now, leave this boring real-world stuff and enter a new realm where magic and
spaceships, thankfully, do exist.

To my
Oma Lorle
you are sorely missed

"It is we ourselves who must answer the questions that life asks of us, and to these questions, we can respond only by being responsible for our existence."

— VIKTOR FRANKL

PART I
A BOY'S DREAM

Chapter One

The storyteller's words transport the boy into a magical realm beyond anything he's ever imagined. Time pauses. He lives a unique experience fabricated just for him. He basks in the glory of blazing golden trees—something that stretches his imagination to the brink. Each word is a drop of paint bringing colour to a grey existence. Every change in timbre is an elixir, filling this boy with life, and he craves more—a starving urchin hankering after a breadcrumb. *More!* He wants so much more.

He becomes the little girl in the tale, homeless just like he is, and feels her bravery course through his soul. It is he who stands up to the looters, refusing to give an inch, and it is he who, moments later, meets the majestic creature of legend. Great scales shimmer, their iridescence cascading over the giant form, and he hears the gong sound, a voice reverberating through his being.

He listens, enraptured. Her words flow—a tugging current drawing him ever deeper into unchartered territory. The small inflections in her voice weave a tapestry of enchanted places, daring adventure, and characters more real than anyone he knows. Mouth half open, the boy leans forward as if getting closer will allow him to take in everything. Immersed as he is, a part of him still wants to know how she does this. How can simple words be so magical?

Then the words end. The spell is broken. Tangible silence spans the interminable moment like a water droplet launching itself from the ceiling of a cave—an eternity encapsulated in a heartbeat—until it lands with an echoing splash. Spectators rouse themselves. The collective breath is followed by cacophony. A cheer goes up for the storyteller, and then patrons turn their attention to what they were doing before the spell drew them in. Deep voices call for ale. Conversations blossom. Laughter sparkles. So much noise jars the silence into a fragmented memory.

The sound of wood scraping on stone brings the boy fully out of his trance. He blinks, pulling himself back to the brightness he'd forgotten while listening to the magical voice of the woman who now rises. Her short cape whirls, adding flair to her movement. His eye is drawn to the flamboyant hat, complete with a bobbing feather. This storyteller is a true master of her craft. She dresses the part, and every action is precise—a holistic display of everything the boy knows a weaver of tales should be. She steps into a darkened alcove and commands a serving girl with an authoritative flick of her hand.

Watching from across the room, he observes the fabler while she picks at the stew she's been served. On occasion, distaste flits across her features as she separates bits of gristle from her meal. The sight of food, together with the fragrant steam wafting from the kitchen, is too much for the boy. His stomach rumbles. It's a loud and prolonged echo. He cringes, hoping others won't be alerted to his presence.

He glances about. The furtive gesture is accompanied by a sigh of relief. No one has a care for the boy hunching in the shadows by the tavern door. He's close enough to the door to escape, should his presence become a problem, but is also near enough to the raised platform where the storyteller performed, and he knows he missed nothing from his vantage point.

The boy returns his attention to the storyteller. Anxiety and excitement meld in his stomach. He watches her push the bowl away and dab at her lips with a handkerchief. He stirs. Determination pools within him. This is his moment. He must make his move or forever regret not doing so. He takes a faltering step forward. His hand trembles and he strains against the sudden weight of his feet. *Move!* He commands. *I have to get there. I must.*

As he approaches, one hesitant motion after another, her gaze locks onto him. Sharp violet eyes pierce him. His courage scurries into some deep recess of his inner self, and he freezes. His eyes widen, and his heart beats faster than the boisterous rhythm of the tavern's patrons. His stomach clenches and pearlescent beads shimmer into existence along his hairline—fire and ice combined into searing droplets of unease.

With inordinate effort, he inhales. Air rasps in his throat. He clenches his jaw, feels the sensation of muscles and tendons working, fuelling his determination. More force allows him to drag forth his courage from its hiding place in the shadows. *I will do this.*

He crosses the room in three bold strides and doesn't drop his gaze from the bewitching violet eyes. He slides onto the bench opposite the storyteller. She's older than he imagined. Her visage is defined by many lines. Her skin is dark, burned by the suns of the empire's many planets, although he imagines her original tone is close to walnut. Long fingers grace her thin hands. Soft veins and hard tendons form ridges across them. He glances up into her violet gaze—so unusual and captivating.

Silence grows between them. The boy is aware of her scrutiny. He feels grimy and wipes a hand on the once-grey homespun of his tunic. Now it's streaked with brown. He knows he's thin and wonders if that will be an advantage or not. Her gaze lingers on his hair, and he instinctively brushes a hand over it, surprised to find it matted. A tickling drip gathers in his nose and travels right to the tip. He sniffs it away.

"Yes?" the storyteller's voice is sharp. "Surely you did not cross the room only to sit there."

The boy drops his gaze. He begins picking at dry grass seeds that cling to his trousers.

"Boy," she continues, "spit it out. I shan't bite." Her voice softens as she speaks, and he looks up again, noting a glint of humour. "Speak," she encourages again, her lips quirking at the corners.

His mouth is dry. He swallows and dampens his lips with the tip of his tongue. With his insides quivering, he gathers his courage by the scruff of the neck and forces it out, blurting, "Teach me! I want to learn. I've always wanted to learn." She stiffens, so he adds, "Mrs Storyteller, I need to be able to tell stories the way you do. I have to know how you do it. Take me as your apprentice. Please."

His lips close, sealing the path of his impassioned speech, cutting off the opportunity for any more to spill out, because the woman shakes her head. The feather on her hat dances at the movement. "I do not take apprentices," she states with finality.

She rises. She's taller than he thought, thin and wiry. His heart plummets at her words. Before his disappointment comes crashing in around him, he pulls together what he can and asks, "What is your name?"

The storyteller steps into the light. "I am Viola Alerion." She bows, flicking her russet cloak with a flourish. Then she turns and walks off.

He sits, stunned. A cocktail of thoughts and emotions whirls through him, that name echoing in his mind as he watches the empire's greatest known storyteller slip out of sight. "No wonder I was so moved," he murmurs. He becomes more acutely aware of his dirtiness; he stands and slinks out of the crowded room. *No wonder she doesn't want anything to do with me. What was I even thinking?*

He steps out into darkness and braces himself against the buffeting wind. With his head bowed, the boy fights against the air to get to another building a short distance away. Sand abrades his exposed hands and cheeks. He seeks shelter in the first doorway that presents itself. The building's deeper darkness comforts him as he shakes particles from his clothes and hair.

When his eyes grow accustomed to the dimness, he sees a row of sleek transports. Foreign things he has little knowledge of. Unfamiliar, hard lines mark these engines of motion. He runs a hand over the sleek surface, feels the cold seeping into his fingers. A peculiar word pops into his mind. *Hover car*. He scratches his head. *Why would I think that?* He doesn't even know what it means. How could he know this thing with the hard casing is a *hover car*?

He shakes his head again. Strange things have been happening since he began this journey. He knows something important is afoot, but he doesn't know what. He thinks on his decision to leave his past behind, to escape that place where he didn't belong and where all eyes bored their disappointment into him. Since leaving the community where he was allowed to live but was never welcomed, he's been sensing the names of things when he encounters them for the very first time.

He glances once more at the row of machines, then walks further into the dimness. He makes out a darker shadow to his left, the outline of a doorway, leading from the carport to a world more familiar to him. As he steps through the rectangle, the boy's nose is assaulted by the odour of manure and hay. His eyes pick out stalls in the half-light. He's met with the swish of a tail, followed by the stamp of a hoof. Shavings shift softly under the weight of a horse, and then a loud snort emanates from one stall.

The boy relaxes. He's accustomed to animals, knows what they're all about. As he passes, a silky muzzle nudges his shoulder over a stall door. He pauses to run a hand over the creature's face, his fingers tingling on the short hairs brushing beneath them. Warmth suffuses his fingertips. Rubbing a little harder, he delights in the animal's nudging response. Life. Warmth. These are the important things.

He continues on his way until he comes to an empty stall. He checks around him, making sure he's alone with the beasts of burden before slipping inside and settling down on a pile of clean shavings. The boy pulls to him a leather bag from behind the trough that's in a corner of the stable and rummages inside. His fingers clasp around a smooth round object, and he pulls out a small apple, breathing in its scent. He takes a bite. The explosion of flavourful pulp and mouth-watering juice makes his stomach growl again. It only takes a few more bites to leave nothing more than a stalk which he tosses over his shoulder. His stomach gurgles, not satisfied with the small offering.

His thoughts buzz around the evening and everything that happened. *I met Viola Alerion!* A smile plays across his lips at the memory of her tale and how he felt when he was there, experiencing the adventure himself. She's everything and more than he imagined. All those times he crept up to the clanspeople as they sat around the fire and shared stories in the flickering light, their voices carrying on the night air—none of it compares to this master fabler. Her ability is in a league of its own, and he knows it, appreciates the depth of her art and longs to be able to weave words in the same way.

Then his dilemma comes crashing into his consciousness. *Can I really give up now?* He ponders how he can convince her that he must be her apprentice. How does he make her see this is important? He trembles at the thought of bothering her again. What will he do if she becomes angry? *Should I even approach her tomorrow?*

A new thought filters through. *Have faith.* The boy shifts, sitting cross-legged and closing his eyes. His heartbeat slows while he focuses on the thought. *Faith. I must have faith in this meeting.*

"Thank you, Mother-Father for this opportunity," he murmurs. "I know you must have contrived this introduction for me, to fulfil my wish to become a storyteller in my own right. Thank you for the many words you've given me and for deeming me worthy of becoming apprenticed to such a great master." Opening his eyes, he then rolls up into a ball, and whispers to himself, "No more doubts. Tomorrow, I try again."

Chapter Two

Viola sits up in the bed and swings her legs over the edge. She rubs the dryness from her eyes and stretches. "This is hopeless," she murmurs. *No more sleep for me*. She stretches again.

Knowing she has limited time to get away from this place, she rises and goes about her morning routine. Tepid water soothes her skin as she allows her mind to play the memory of the boy who came to her the evening before. His impassioned request haunted her all night, along with the memory of his gaunt, drawn face and the blazing longing in his eyes.

No matter now; what is done is done. Viola needs to leave as soon as possible. She knows they're but a day behind her. It wouldn't do to drag someone like him into all of this. *It is better this way—at least, it will be better for him.*

Still, the brightness of those chestnut eyes resurfaces

in her memory. *I used to burn with that passion for tales—Once, a long, long time ago.* She grimaces and turns her attention to the task at hand. With forceful motions, she pushes her legs into simple trousers, and a drab brown shirt follows, smooth fabric slipping against her skin. While she buttons the shirt, she notices the papery dryness of her hands. *Nothing to be done about that. Not now, at any rate.*

Sighing, she folds her colourful storyteller garb into small squares and slips it into a large backpack. With a deft wave of one hand, the flamboyant hat shrinks to a third of its size and she places it in a box that also makes its way into the backpack. She glances about. *Got everything.*

Palest light begins filtering through cracks along the shutters. "No time to waste," she mutters.

A short while later, Viola steps out into the cool greyness of pre-dawn. She glances about her, eyes alert and questing. The cluster of buildings making up the roadside inn is still with the sleepiness of first light. There are three buildings. The two-story inn where she performed and slept, a separate block off to the side for the outhouse, and opposite her, a building that houses modes of transportation.

She's relieved there's no one about. The relief sparks a glimmer of hope that her performance last evening will serve as a decoy and confuse her pursuers about her whereabouts.

A furtive motion draws her attention to the building across from the inn where she stands. A figure shifts in the shadows of the carport doorway. Squinting to see better, she observes that it's a small individual. She meets the gaze of the boy from the previous evening, and her heart clenches. Viola wants to take him with her, but instead, she shakes her head in a decisive motion that brooks no contradiction. She struggles to counter the voice clamouring within her, calling for her to hear him out.

Viola shakes her head once again—more to silence her conscience than to reiterate her decision from the night before. She hefts the rucksack onto her back and steps out into the dusty road. Her steps are brisk. A powerful purpose drives her onwards, and soon the inn's few buildings slip into the horizon behind her while the growing light illuminates the ochre countryside. In the distance, running at an angle and crossing her path, Viola makes out the hazy shimmer of mountains. They're very far distant. Between her and those far-flung crags stretch miles and miles of yellow-brown rock and sand speckled with greyish shrubs.

After some time walking only to the rhythm of her sturdy boots on the grainy path, Viola becomes aware of someone behind her. She glances over her shoulder and manages to make out a faint figure following. She confirms that it's only one, but still, her heart speeds up. She looks back at short intervals. *Have they already caught up with me? Was yesterday's performance all in vain?*

She picks up her pace, checking behind her again while fear gnaws at her. As the figure maintains the distance between them and remains alone, she relaxes her strides. "Confounded boy!"

A few crunching steps later, she relents and slows her pace. A rough chuckle escapes her. *Well, at least he is determined.* An approving smile twitches into existence.

The boy closes the distance between them, and Viola takes the opportunity to scrutinise him. He's scrawny, with tangled hair reaching below his earlobes. She estimates his age at around thirteen. As he draws closer, she considers his clothing. He wears sandals of dark leather. There's something lopsided about them; they're solid, but an odd shape. *Handmade,* she thinks. The grey sheep's wool of his clothes is roughly woven, and the cut of his trousers and shirt is simple. *Vestment of a time gone by*, she muses. A leather satchel bounces at his hip, hanging from a strap he wears across his chest.

He draws up beside her, and they fall into step together. He beams up at her and says, his voice bright and youthful, "Thank you, Master. You're kind to wait."

Viola snorts, unable to hold back her irritability, and snaps, "I am not your master. I do not take apprentices. I never have, and I never shall. You should go back to whatever hole spawned you."

Unperturbed, the boy replies, "I can't go back."

Viola senses weight in the words. She doesn't want to know about his burdens. *We all face hardships.* However, in spite of herself, there's something about the determination in his gaze that makes her ask, "And why is that?"

He shrugs. The motion is both heavy and dismissive. "I don't belong there."

"Well." She pauses, unsure of what to say. Then, trying to infuse her words with kindness while remaining firm, she adds, "You certainly do not belong with me, either."

In answer, his face creases into a knowing smile. "But I do. I left that place to see the world and find a storyteller to teach me. The first storyteller I met is you, Viola Alerion, the greatest master storyteller in the empire." Viola's heart constricts at the fervour in his voice. "I don't believe this is a coincidence," he continues. "The great Mother-Father answered my prayers and sent me to you. I'll do their bidding as I've always done."

She rolls her eyes. *Not only a harebrained youth but a fanatic as well. What have I got myself into?* Aloud, she reiterates, "I have nothing against us travelling together. The roads are open to all, so that is up to you. Nevertheless, as I said before, I shall not take on an apprentice. Believe me; you will be glad of it in the long run. You do not want to associate with me."

She meets his wide-eyed gaze. She strains to put weight into her eyes, forcing him to accept her decision, but instead, he shrugs and quips, "You'll see. This is meant to be. Our meeting is blessed by the Holy Parent, which is more powerful than either of us."

"I don't want to hear any more ridiculous nonsense about gods and pre-destiny. I don't believe in that hogwash." Exasperated, she watches the boy bite down on his lower lip, trying, unsuccessfully, to hide a smile.

The two continue trudging in silence, their gazes drawn to the vastness of the landscape and the endlessness of the road they walk. Viola gauges the time from the suns' positions in the sky. *That should be far enough*, she thinks. Without warning, she veers right and steps off the track. She observes the boy beside her who acknowledges the strangeness of her behaviour with the slightest lift of one eyebrow. He says nothing though, and although Viola notices curiosity burning behind his eyes, he has the forbearance not to ask.

The going is tougher through the sandy soil of the scrublands. Viola pushes on as the red sun climbs high into the pale blue canopy above, washing out the colour to a watery hint of azure. The washed-out-yellow sun, the second, follows its companion's trajectory. It's hot, and there's nowhere to take refuge. The bushes are knee-high, their tiny grey-green leaves dotting the thin branches. The scrub is a study in grey and brown and yellow, a painting in which the artist has splattered his brushwork in impressionistic dabs of subdued hues.

Heat sears off the ground, blasting Viola and her companion with waves of shimmering incandescence. She knows they need to find shelter soon, but still, she pushes on. She glances behind them, but the landscape is equally flat and dotted with low vegetation in all directions. They're alone.

Turning her attention forward once more, Viola picks out a tree in the distance. It's spindly and offers little shade, but she knows it's the only refuge they'll find in this godforsaken place. They reach their perfunctory haven as the white-hot disk peaks at its zenith.

Viola wipes her glistening face and damp dustiness soaks into her cotton handkerchief. She takes a look at the boy. His breathing is fast, and he looks a little ill. His face is gaunt, cheeks hollow. A realisation strikes her.

"You have not eaten today, have you?"

The tiniest shake of his head confirms her suspicion. She rummages in her pack and pulls out a loaf of bread and some cheese. Removing a knife from her belt, she combines a chunk of each and hands them to him.

He hesitates, but she encourages him by gesturing the rough sandwich towards him. Forgetting her own hunger, Viola watches him devour what she offered. Her heart goes out to him, this small and frail child that he is. *What story might lie here?*

She cuts off her empathetic musings. *That is a highway to trouble. Don't get involved; don't get attached.* She thinks on the nature of her situation and knows she must stay level-headed, for the sake of this boy, if not for herself. She knows it's better for him in the long run because she's a wanted woman. Her conscience couldn't bear it if she dragged him into her mess.

Licking the last creamy remnants from his fingers, the boy looks up, casting his huge brown eyes on Viola. She feels the cold shell she's spent years honing softening from the inside out, and she feels threatened by the change. Her mouth presses into a sour line. "You should not have followed after me." She takes a bite of food and glares at him.

He grins at her. There's mischief in his eyes. "But Master, it was the best thing I could have done! I got real food for the first time in days!"

Viola can't help herself. Laughter bubbles up from a hidden recess she's almost forgotten existed. The next thing she knows, she's choking on a breadcrumb. The boy is beside her, rubbing her back. He pulls her water flask from a side-pocket in her backpack. She drinks.

Once she breathes easily again, the atmosphere between them turns serious. Viola breaks the weight of it by asking, "So, how did you come to be here?"

His eyes light up, stars glimmering in dark wells. “Does that mean you’ll take me on as your apprentice?” Hope resonates in his voice. He quivers with excitement.

Viola shakes her head. There’s no malice. It’s a simple fact, but still, she feels guilt when she sees disappointment clouding his face. An urgent need to explain races through her and she stumbles over her words to make things at least a little right. ”I— I just don’t. I mean—” She huffs her frustration, then starts again, irritable forcefulness driving the words out. ”I am not good at it. I am no teacher, and I don’t want company. I travel alone. That is all there is to it.”

The boy nods, but Viola detects a hint of willfulness in the set of his jaw. Before she can confirm her decision, reiterate that it’s impossible, his expression changes. She falters, unable to insist that her mind is made up.

A mischievous glint replaces his stubbornness as he says, ”My story will have to wait then, Master.”

Viola shrugs. ”In that case, I shall take a nap. It is better to stay out of the direct sun at this time of day.” She shuts her eyes, cutting off the monotonous vision of Mshrali’s dust bowl, this semi-arid expanse ringed by hazy cliffs where people think twice before setting foot. Her nap takes her away from the dry heat to a place where fountains tinkle in the glow of a single sun.

Some time later, Viola's eyelids flutter. In those moments between sleeping and waking, she hears an unfamiliar scuffling sound. Her eyes fly open as she comes to her feet in one swift motion, followed by the need to double up when pain shoots through her leg. She sees the boy walking towards her, carrying an armful of sticks from the local flora.

Her fright turns into irritation. "What are you doing?"

The boy drops his load at her feet and looks up. Intelligence burns in his brown eyes. "A drone passed by a while ago. I thought it would be useful to have head-coverings that help us blend into the environment when seen from above."

Viola frowns. Her already shaken nerves are jarred by the way he says the word drone, hesitant yet emphasising the word, as though it's new and unfamiliar to him. "How do you even know what a drone is? They are not common in this backwater."

He shrugs. In the way he holds himself, Viola detects a level of discomfort she can't place. His eyes are on his dusty toes now, but then, again, they flick up to hers, and his gaze becomes piercing. "It's by knowing things that I survive."

Viola gapes. Is there anything she can say to that? What does it mean? What does it say about this boy? She realises there's far more to this youth than she could ever have imagined. Her prejudices have blinded her to how different he is. *Who seeks out a wandering storyteller in this day and age, anyway?*

She shakes her head, clearing the sandstorm of her thoughts. *I need to let this settle,* she thinks and promises herself that for the time they journey together, she'll observe this boy more closely. She takes stock of their surroundings. The second sun's disk has descended from its midday perch and no longer blisters with its blinding light. The boy sits with his back against the tree trunk. His fingers weave out a pattern of stubby branches and leafy twigs, and Viola sinks to the ground, mesmerised by the motions.

Within a few minutes, he's contrived a bush with a hollow at the bottom so it can serve as a hat. Viola pauses in her thoughts—*headdress.* He holds out his creation to her. It's ridiculous, but his words play in her mind. *It's by knowing things that I survive.* She holds back her derision. She might very well be able to learn a thing or two from his pragmatic ways. He could be really useful to have around. Then she stops herself. *No, no, Vi. This is the first step. It is too dangerous, and too much is at stake.*

The boy proffers his rudimentary headdress to her again, and this time Viola takes it. Unable to conceal her distaste, she dons the fake bush. He returns to his work and doesn't even look at her while he creates a second one. Viola feels her cheeks crease into a smile. *At least he is hard-working.*

Realisation hits her. "You have not told me your name."

The lightness in his manner gusts away on her words. He shrinks, folds in on himself. His whisper is so low that Viola is forced to lean forward in her attempt to catch what he says. "I left it behind when I departed on this journey."

She feels her face contort. "What does that mean?"

Silence draws out between them. Then he looks up. His voice is firm. "When I left the clan, I renounced my right to the name they gave me. You may call me what you wish." Then he returns his attention to the twigs in his lap.

The whole conversation takes Viola into the world of her past. She recalls the moment, so many years before, when she chose to follow the yearning of her heart and set foot on the road. She hears the anger in a beloved voice, the determination in the haughty eyes that brook no contradiction. *"If you choose this path, you are no longer my daughter."* In the faint place of her nostalgia, Viola remembers another name she was once called before she started out, one so long forgotten that she failed to recollect the pain that went with the loss.

She returns to the moment, and her heart goes out to

this boy. "I understand," she offers. *Small consolation,* she thinks. *It is a terrible pain to be an outcast.*

The boy finishes his camouflage hat, and they set off into the heat of the afternoon. The two travellers walk in silence, each absorbed in the world of their own thoughts, mimicking the mute orbs tracing out an arc above them. The heat thickens the air, and no breeze offers a respite from the oppressiveness.

Time passes until the boy grabs Viola's hand and whispers, "A drone is coming."

He hunkers down on his haunches, sitting very still. Viola can't hear anything but is loath to look up for fear of giving themselves away. She follows his lead and kneels, so her head is even with the shrubbery around them. A moment passes in absolute silence, except for the overwhelming pounding of her heart. Then she hears the soft whirr of an engine above them. It makes several passes but doesn't stop, and Viola's ears pick up the boy's sigh of relief when the tool of the empire buzzes out of earshot.

Paralysed by their terror of discovery, they remain crouched where they are before glancing up and confirming that the machine really is gone.

"We must hurry," Viola says. "We need to get out of this area and leave as little sign as possible of our passing."

He nods, and she notices his eyes narrow in response

to some pointed thought. Then his face smooths again, and he walks beside her in silence. Realising she's holding her breath, Viola allows the air to escape. She's relieved he hasn't voiced his thoughts or asked her why the drone is searching for her, but she knows she may have to explain the situation should the hunt continue.

She shakes her head and decides to lose him in the next settlement. *It is safer if he doesn't know anything. Otherwise, they will be after him too.*

A brooding silence draws out between them. They walk through the dusty landscape, heat pouring from them in the afternoon glow. Ochre particles settle onto all exposed flesh, turning them the same pale brown as the desert. Viola strides forward, her motions swift, until she realises she's walking alone. She looks back. The boy struggles to keep up, but he doesn't complain. She slows her pace again, her eyes flicking to the azure canopy above or glancing out over the still, brown landscape behind them.

The second sun sinks to the horizon, bathing in its glow everything it touches. The yellow-brown earth turns a vibrant gold in the evening light. The mountains remain purple, far-distant. Viola shifts her position to keep their darkening shadow in line with her right shoulder. Night falls, and they keep walking. She can tell the boy is fatigued. *He insisted on coming with me. He will just have to keep up or find his own way, as he has before this.*

In the dimness, Viola makes out a lighter expanse cutting through the vegetation in an unnatural line. "At last," she mutters. Turning to the boy, she adds, "Come, there is a farm near here. We can seek shelter there for the night."

He nods, and they walk along the compacted dirt road until the stars light up the cobalt heavens. A sliver of soft yellow lights up the Eastern expanse and the moon bathes the landscape's globular bushes in eerie light. The going is easier on the road, and their pace quickens.

A short distance away, a series of black shadows loom into view. The buildings are dark. No light twinkles; deserted inkiness and silence are all that meets them. Viola pauses at a half-tumbled down fence and stretches out her awareness. "I cannot sense any living thing," she says.

"There's still shelter, right?"

Viola nods, and they approach the nearest edifice. The door is solid, but shifts when she puts her weight against it. It opens onto what was once a barn. Derelict stalls stand empty—gaping black expanses where life once found shelter. Casting about her, she takes in a sturdy wooden ladder up to a loft. She grunts her satisfaction and drops the heavy pack onto the ground at her feet. "I am going to check the house, but I think we can seek our refuge here without any trouble."

She heads back outside and crosses the dirt courtyard to the house. Her approach is tentative, gauging the darkness and the silence. Her first impression is the door that hangs loose on one of its hinges. Peeking inside from her vantage point, Viola can only make out varying shades of grey and black. She's certain the place is abandoned, but knowing the door is damaged, she returns to the barn. Her instinct was right. At least they can close the barn door and keep out any unwanted night visitors. The bush is filled with nocturnal creatures.

Returning, she pushes with all her might, heaving against disuse and rust, and finally closes the door, which screeches in protest. She turns to her pack and rummages inside, pulling out a cold object from within. Muttering under her breath, she watches as faint pink light glows into existence, revealing a large crystal. She notes the boy's curiosity and offers him the light.

He reaches out and touches it, then lifts the crystal from her palm. "How does it do that?"

"It is a simple spell, binding light into rock to be released at will," Viola smiles. His vibrant curiosity is contagious. "This one is lamplight trapped in quartz. Other, more powerful ones use sunlight."

"It's pretty."

She nods and looks about. The ladder up to the loft seems solid. "It will probably be best to sleep up there," and she points into the darkened recess.

The boy makes his way over and tests the ladder, his hand glowing with the quartz he still holds. He climbs up, and Viola follows to discover a small alcove. *Better than sleeping out in the cold*, she thinks before a violent sneeze assaults her. In the light of the lustrous quartz, she sees a dust halo swirl around the boy.

They settle down, and Viola prepares a frugal meal. The boy thanks her, after performing what she considers a disappearing act with his food. One moment she's handing him the bread with cheese and the next, he's licking his fingers and picking for crumbs in his shirt.

Chewing more slowly, she savours the creamy texture of the cheese as it melds with the soft centre of the bread and contrasts with the crust. Simple but wholesome. Bread and cheese, the flavours of life on the road.

Viola observes the boy. She's struck by an idea, and without thinking, she inquires, "So you have decided you want to be my apprentice. You proved some of your worth today, but what of storytelling? Do you have any talent at all?"

He blinks, then grins. "I can try. What would you like to hear?"

Viola smiles grim sweetness back at him. "What do you dare serve me?"

He takes a moment to collect his thoughts, and Viola notes his introspection. *Good. He is taking this very seriously.* She's satisfied that at least he shows his determination, but at the same time, she wonders whether it's wrong to give him hope.

Shifting, he adjusts himself on the hard planks flooring their place of shelter and begins.

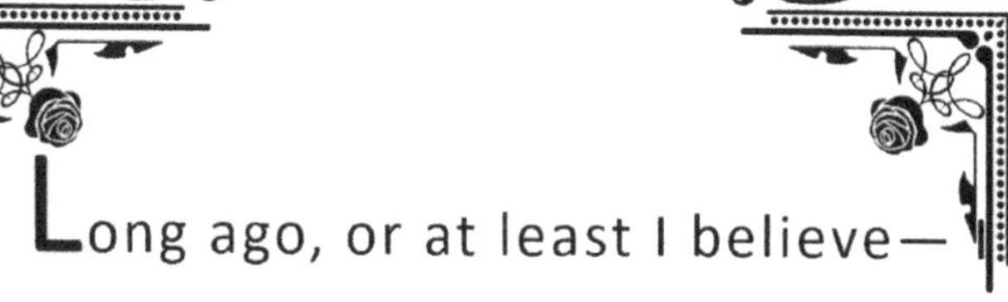

Long ago, or at least I believe—mean I've been told it was long ago—On a planet far away in a distant galaxy there lived a race of humans blessed by the Great Parent. Unlike other humans, the use of magic was not restricted to women. Those with magical abilities were powerful beyond imagining and could bend the elements to their will—and even cross vast distances in the blink of an eye. They were a people of wonder, and their world was something to behold. But among them lived those who had no magical powers and who resented them their magical abilities. The Terrans, as the people from that planet are called, began to lose their way and forgot the teachings of their parent-deity, the Mother-Father who protected and cared for them.

These people cared nothing for the godly gift of their world and exploited the resources of their planet until they risked the destruction of all life there. Other living creatures were pushed to the brink of extinction, and the natural world fell out of balance. Realising they couldn't stem the tide caused by greed, the Terran magicians created enormous spaceships to save the knowledge they'd acquired and to spread the teachings of the Great Parent in other worlds. They wanted to stop a similar catastrophe

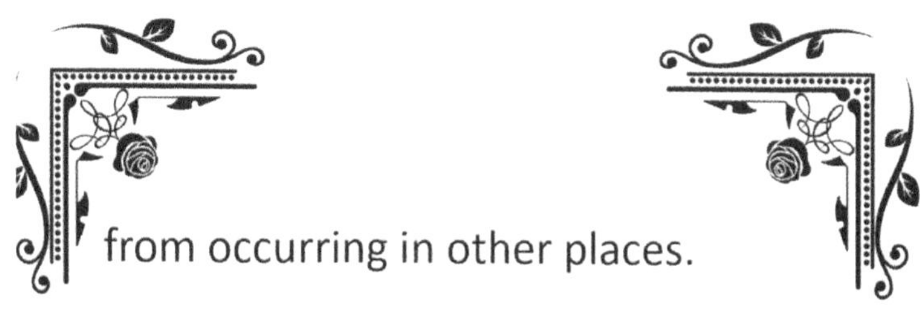

from occurring in other places.

The spaceships travelled for a long, long time and at last, found other planets inhabited by humans. They even came to this Haldrian Empire and small communities settled in different places, teaching their message of love and grace from the Holy Creator and the warning not to lose one's way by yielding to greed and destruction. They used their magic to stabilise nature, preventing it from falling out of balance, and they taught others the message from the Great Parent. And—

"Stop!" Viola exclaims. "That will do. I shall tell you my decision in the morning."

She pulls her russet cloak from her pack and rolls

over, not even waiting for the boy to close his mouth or nod. While she lies there, feigning sleep, knots fetter her insides. Viola chides herself for her abruptness but can't stop the bothered hammering of her heart. *What a strange topic for him to choose. What was that odd story all about?* She's never heard anything of the like and her jaw clenches, teeth grinding against each other. She isn't used to being surprised and wonders why this story caught her off guard. There's also the strange flicker of power to consider. She's intrigued by what she saw: rainbow shimmers dancing around him as he spoke. *What does that mean?* Deep down, somewhere in her gut, she knows this is important. There's something significant about this young boy who's run away from home. Should she accept his request and make him her apprentice?

Her rational mind scatters out its many counterarguments, but what she saw gives her no rest. There's nothing for it; she'll have to give in and see where this adventure takes her. With the decision made, Viola slips into a tranquil sleep where she dreams of beautiful things long buried.

Chapter Three

The boy glances out over the countryside. Something is different about the landscape. Although the same flat expanse stretches out before him, dotted with bushes that reach between his knees and his waist, there's something odd about what he sees now compared to what he did several weeks ago. When this journey with Viola began, everything was either ochre or greyish-brown. Now the ground is off-colour with a purplish hue, and the plants have bright green veins popping out of their leaves. A shiver crawls down his spine.

"Did I tell you to stop?" Viola's sharp voice cuts into his thoughts.

"No, Master. Apologies!"

"Start from the beginning. Don't get distracted, boy."

He nods, wiping sweat from his brow, and recounts the tale Viola has been teaching him. Every evening she recites a short story or a segment of a longer one. Over the course of every day, he's expected to repeat it, bearing with her never-ending corrections until he can reproduce it flawlessly. On this afternoon, he recounts *The Sewing Princess*. Most of the tales capture his attention, but this one doesn't, and he struggles to bring it to life the way Viola does.

At length, she exclaims, "Of all the confounded fools! What was I thinking when I agreed to teach you?"

She's irritable, and he feels responsible. "I'm sorry, Master. I just don't get this one. It makes no sense. What is it about?"

"What do you mean? What does that have to do with your ability to recount it?"

"When I don't understand something, I can't get behind it, and you can hear I'm not into this one. Maybe another will be better?"

"Oh? So, are you ready to give up?"

He frowns. "No! It might just be easier with a different tale."

"Did you choose to become a storyteller because you think it is easy?" her voice is deadly.

"No, I didn't mean it like that." He pauses, assessing the intensity of her displeasure and then adds, "I'm sorry,

Master. I'll keep trying until I get it right." Her only reply is a grunt. He continues with a soft, "Thank you, Master," in the hope of appeasing her.

A short while later, they come to a cluster of shacks sprinkled between the road and a pond. A few children sit in the shade offered by overhanging roofs. They make no sound. The boy wonders what ails them and the hairs on his arms prickle. They're listless, and their eyes are hollow, and his gut clenches at the sight. Viola stops at the first building and speaks to the only visible adult, a wizened old man with but a few teeth. His weather-beaten visage reveals the harshness of the life he's lived.

"Good afternoon," Viola begins bowing her head. "We seek shelter from the midday heat. Would your village be able to offer us any?"

The man turns his head, and the boy sees milk-white eyes staring out into nothingness. "There's nothing but ruin and death here," the man rasps. "All those who could have left. Go, while you're still able. There's nothing but oblivion here."

Ice stabs through the boy's veins and a multitude of shivers convulse him, making it impossible to hear the storyteller's reply. Uneasiness settles in the pit of his stomach, and he begins to back away.

Viola strides from the village. She's beside him and appears unaffected by the situation. He glances up at her, but her face is unreadable. When the village lies some way behind, he ventures, "What of those children?"

Viola's jaw twitches. "Their death sentence was signed when the others left the settlement. They were probably abandoned because they had the sickness. Being struck by the blight is certain death."

He shudders.

After close to another hour of trudging, they see one lone tree off the road. Taking shelter under the sparse shade, the boy begins once more with his tale, but he falters after less than a minute. He glances back the way they've travelled. The cluster of houses is well out of sight, but his mind continues to drag the image of that place of doom before his eyes. It swims into view, superimposed over the shimmering panorama.

He stands, conviction coursing through him. "We have to go back. They can't just be left to die out there."

Viola pulls him into a tight embrace. She holds him until tears well up, spilling from him in a silent howl. "The blight has taken them," she murmurs. "There is nothing to be done, and all you will get for going back is to catch it too." When the flow of his sobs ebbs, she adds, "It is admirable that you care so much. Hold onto that. It is rare in this empire. Do not let the horrors you encounter diminish your humanity."

He nods, not trusting his voice. Gazing out over the bushes, hints of luminescence on their leaves, he observes the corrupting purple that blankets the earth around them. "What is wrong with this place?"

One of Viola's eyebrows curves into her forehead. "You mean you have never encountered the blight before?" When he shakes his head, she says, "This planet is overrun by it. There are few places that are not affected. Anyone living a long time in a blight-stricken region will succumb to illness. The area we are in shows mild signs of blight. How don't you know this?"

The question pulls his mind into a memory that's filled with gentleness. He remembers how his family used to work. His father and sister side by side, her charcoal hair gleaming in the suns as she wove her fingers through the air. Their voices raised in song as they moved up the hillside bordering the farmstead. Other members of the clan dotting the entire valley, walking and motioning with their arms, singing about purity and wholesomeness. *They were cleaning the air and purifying the earth.* The realisation comes as a surprise. *I always knew it was important, but the purpose was never clear.*

His thoughts return to the offish-purple in the sand and to Viola's question. He gathers himself before replying. "My family dedicated their time to cleaning it. I didn't understand then, but now I realise that was why we moved so often, going from one place to another. It was to purify the natural world."

"How? The blight is untreatable."

The boy bites his lip. *Can't say too much. That could be dangerous.* "I don't know. I wasn't able to do it." He sees curiosity spark in Viola's eyes, but he shakes his head, looking at her meaningfully. "I was never like them. I can't do what they can."

Viola frowns, but before she can say anything, they hear a rustle in the bush a short distance away. They both look up. A thin creature, the same shade as the sand, sits on its haunches, front paws lifted to its chest. It's around two handspans high and looks straight at them with its pointy face. Then it raises its dark snout and lets out a chattering call.

A pause follows in which the animal turns its attention back to the boy and Viola. He feels a shiver run up his spine when he notices the creature's eyes. They're bright yellow, and they glow. His ears pick out the sound of answering chatters from all over the scrub, and he feels the hairs on the back of his neck rise.

Within moments, they're surrounded by more of the knee-high creatures. There are dozens of them, all rushing up to a distance of a few yards and then sitting back on their haunches, watching, waiting. With a shudder, he sees their ears, tails and paws are a violent shade of purple.

The boy's attention is drawn to Viola, who is rummaging in her pack. Her face is frantic and redoubles his sense of foreboding. He glances back at the creatures. Some of them are drooling, others foaming at the mouth. Their stance is menacing, and their sandy-brown coats are tattered, tufts missing in places, as though they're wont to fight.

Voice trembling at an unbidden thought, he asks, "Are we food?" His hands shake. He's a leaf buffeted by the winds of fear, being tugged towards the abyss where terror will consume him.

Viola pulls out a four-inch bamboo stick and meets his gaze. Her expression is grim. "Yes." She starts twisting at the stick, pulling a section out and lengthening it to four times the size. As she does so, she explains. "Blight-struck meerkats like the taste of meat. In a few moments, we shall have a mob, a hundred strong, descending upon us, lusting after our flesh. They will rip and tear at our bodies until we succumb to blood loss and then they will feast on us until nothing but white bones remain."

The grim, matter-of-fact way she says it is hair-raising. *She's seen someone go that way.* Another shudder tears through him.

Viola swings the now waist-high stick about her in a practised flurry. Her expression is fierce. Then she slips the quartz crystal from her pocket and fastens it to one end of the staff. The boy watches the stone glow and wonders what help it might be, but he finds the gleam in her eyes somewhat reassuring.

A violent screech goes up, sending chills knifing into the boy's already petrified insides. He's paralysed as he watches wave upon wave of the creatures scurrying towards the tree where he stands beside Viola. She shoves him towards the tree trunk, and he loses his balance, tumbling against the sturdy column, bark scraping his cheek. "Stay there!" she orders. "Don't get in my way."

She whirls her staff in an arc, creating around her a glowing crescent of shimmering light. The first meerkat launches itself into the air, a wild shriek coming from its foam-flecked jaws. Its dayglow eyes are fixed on Viola.

The boy watches, heart pounding in his throat, as Viola lifts her stick and catches the animal across the abdomen. It hurtles to the ground and lands with a soft thump next to the boy's foot, and a cry strangles in his throat. He can't tear his eyes from the limp form in front of him. The mad luminescence has disappeared from the creature's eyes, which are now a glazed black. His brain focuses on details—the unnatural angle at which the creature's hind leg lies twisted, the utter stillness of this broken body as it lies on the ground, a pink tinge creeping into the saliva and staining its small teeth.

Faced with the death of this tiny animal, a knife

twists in the boy's heart. His mind runs a course of thoughts sharp and focused, but also detached from what is happening around him. He hears the stern voice of his father. "The sanctity of life is something precious that must be guarded." Yet, here he is, a boy of thirteen, faced with *kill or be killed*. Panic fills him. He knows that the fact of this shattered corpse at his feet is wrong. It goes against everything he's learned and believes in.

Viola's staff whirls into his vision, and he's drawn back to the intensity of the moment. He watches her tool of death curve, hitting several creatures and then, as another ten or more of the meerkats leap at her, the crystal at the top of the staff pulsates, sending out a rush of power, hurling all of them out into the scrub. Smashed bodies litter the ground around them, and the boy feels his breath crush him. He sinks to his knees. The horror of the moment pulls him down into a world of nightmare. *It's not supposed to be this way!*

Inside him, something snaps. It's a jarring, irreversible breaking. His eyes fly open. Viola is barely able to keep the mob of crazed animals at bay. She's sweating, and in a flash, he sees desperation in her eyes. She mutters something and raises the staff, leaving herself open to the first row of creatures who seize their moment and bite into her exposed legs. He watches as the staff begins a downward motion.

In that instant, the boy knows she will release a spell so powerful it will blast all the meerkats surrounding them into obliteration. His mind screams. *Care for all living things.*

"Stop!" he bellows.

He's on his feet from the impact of his outburst. His breaths, coming in rapid succession, rasp in his ears. Stillness meets his gaze. Everything is frozen. Viola stands, her staff a hands-breadth above the ground, her short hair plastered to her face. One meerkat hovers in mid-leap; another is frozen with its teeth at the point of ripping through her trousers.

There's absolute silence. The sea of furry creatures has closed in on them—a rising wave stopped right at the crest before it breaks to come crashing onto the beach. Not even a breeze rustles. Only the blazing disks of the two suns witness the boy's feat.

He exhales, then steps between the frozen mass of creatures and removes the staff from Viola's fingers. He lays a hand on her shoulder, and she comes back into motion.

Her arm moves with decisive downward action, the intention of a moment before thwarted by some unknown power. She stops and looks up at the scene of stillness about her. "What the—" she exclaims, confusion sending turmoil through her eyes.

Her gaze falls on the boy, and he lowers his head. "I needed it to stop."

"What—?" Her voice dies. He wonders whether she wanted to say "What needed to stop?" or "What did you do?"

"I needed the killing to stop," he says, stepping through the wave of creatures and putting distance between himself and the limp forms littering the ground.

She folds her arms, irritation glinting in her eyes. "Well, if I had known you could do *this*, I would not have needed to kill any of them. It is not as if I wanted to."

"I didn't know I could do this. I don't even know if it was me who did it," he says gesturing at the frozen creatures. He turns around, away from the carnage. His insides are thawing, but he still doesn't feel like himself: his heart flutters and faintness tugs at his mind. Crouching down and looking out over the land where these creatures live—flat expanse stretching out into the distance—he thinks, *It's their home. We're passers-by, and we didn't respect them as we should. Please, Mother-Father, forgive this transgression.* He bows his head.

"Why aren't you relieved?" Viola asks, her voice uncomprehending and glacial.

"How can you be happy with so much death?" He can't keep the anguish from his voice. Now he's staring her in the eye. "We committed sacrilege against the Great Parent. Care for all living things. That's the teaching I was raised on. I can't rejoice in this loss; I must show I learned my lesson. I won't let something like this happen again—not for my sake." His tirade fades at the look in her eyes. Her face is a blank mask. He falters, then adds, as an afterthought, "This is what I know is right: I must do what I can to avoid the catastrophe that will come with such wilful neglect of the ordinances."

Viola extricates herself from the mob of meerkats now trapped in time. She struggles to get her trouser leg free from the jaws of one overzealous creature. Once liberated, she sets off towards the road and calls over her shoulder, "Please, don't mind me. I have no qualms about living today."

The boy lifts his face heavenward once more and whispers, "Thank you for your guidance and protection. Thank you for your gift of power that saved so much life today. Please give these creatures the gift of your blessing and healing."

He rises to his feet and his eyes cast over the wave of creatures, frozen in their attack. He brushes a fingertip over the nearest purple tail. It's his gesture of remorse. Then he turns and joins Viola on the road.

A ripple passes through a mob of sandy creatures. A whisker twitches, wide staring eyes blink and feral snarls relax. Soft chatter erupts as the animals come to. The warm rays of the red and yellow suns melt away unnatural hues leaving behind sleek beige fur and inquisitive black eyes. Sooty noses twitch this way and that as the mob of meerkats disperses, slinking into the semi-desert of their home in search of grubs and other insects.

Chapter Four

Viola observes the boy—her apprentice. His reaction to the incident with the blight-struck meerkats baffles her. *How is he not moved by what he did? Doesn't he understand the significance of it?* It's beyond comprehension, but she knows, somehow, he stopped the onslaught of the raging creatures merely by willing it so. *Instead of marvelling in wonder, he spouts gibberish about the sanctity of life and begs forgiveness from gods. How can he be so innocent that he doesn't know this is a kill-or-be-killed world?*

She remains absorbed in her thoughts and continues on her way without waiting for him to finish whatever it is he's doing. She just wants to get away from the rabid creatures as quickly as she can. There's also the pressing need to put as much distance as possible between her and that spot because Viola knows the consequences of using magic. It leaves a trail that can be followed. The tree, her shelter less than half an hour ago, has become a beacon, and the empress' hounds will be upon her if she doesn't get out of the area quickly.

Then another thought strikes. *What community can keep a child so sheltered from all the evil in this world? How is it possible he can be this naive? At his age! If he cannot take a few blight-struck animals dying, then any of the other encounters we may have on this journey could break him.* Viola realises she needs to help him through this. He has to understand that the world doesn't work the way he's been taught. It is a harsh place.

Viola casts her gaze about and sees him walking a few paces behind her, absorbed in his thoughts. She clears her throat, and he looks up. When his eyes meet hers, he smiles. It's a small gesture, which Viola reads as "I'm not alright, but in time I will be." *Not good enough,* she thinks.

Her heart squeezes. His slender features and wide eyes give him a vulnerable look; a part of her wants to pull him into her arms and tell him everything will be all right, but she knows that isn't the truth. *The world is a hard place. Mollycoddling will not help him. Right, let us do this.*

A deep breath is all the preparation she allows herself before launching into her explanation. "Boy, you must understand that whatever you learned of the world in your home may not apply in the wider universe. There are things that happen, things that are done, and they are awful. If you allow them to get to you, if you let them grab your heart and squeeze, you will not stand a chance. You will get yourself killed. I want you to understand that survival is the most important thing. You need to do anything you can to make it to tomorrow. Every day is a fight against the horrors of this universe we live in, and I don't want to see you lose. I like your spunk."

He comes to a standstill, observing her. His stance exudes sadness. "It's a poor world, you see, Master."

"What's that supposed to mean?"

He sighs. "You see only death and hatefulness. What about the light? What about beauty? What of all the interconnections that make things happen? What of *circumstance*? We live in a bountiful, abundant Universe. The greater powers always want to help us so that something good can come out of the darkness. Wherever I look, I see opportunities. I know we humans are more powerful than you give us credit for and I know we can all be agents for good."

Viola throws her hands up in the air. "You are delusional, and you are going to get yourself hurt. Your ideas are naive and will make you fall prey to those who would exploit you, do you harm, or simply kill you. Humans are a plague on everything they touch. Greed drives destruction and brings the corruption of all that is good. You need to start using your faculty for reason."

"Master," he replies, his voice full of emotion. "Look around you. What do you see?"

Viola closes her eyes for a second. *Patience,* she admonishes herself. Her eyes open and she takes in the dusty road they've been walking for weeks, the never-ending desert of fruitless bushes and sand stretching out on all sides. The only break in the monotony is the mountains which have grown on the horizon in the time they've been walking. "I see an arid expanse," she says at length.

"They are poor eyes that only see desert and death. Look closer. Look at this bush." He points to a shrub near them and takes a step towards it.

Viola senses her irritation expanding within her, a balloon filling to bursting. Clenching her fists, she stills the urge to snap at him and instead steps forward to look at the bush. Grey sticks fan out. They make for almost bare branches. She has to lean closer to see the tiny sage-coloured leaves.

Heat prickles on her neck and forehead. Viola senses sweat gathering into beads and poising, ready to trickle down her face. She rises to her full height, pulling a handkerchief from her pocket. While she dabs at the sweaty patches on her face and neck, she says, her voice oozing irritability, "What am I supposed to see? There are some sticks with a few leaves on them." The boy's wide-eyed gaze sends her into paroxysms of annoyance. "I don't have time for this! We need to keep moving." She stuffs her dirt-stained handkerchief back into her pocket.

His voice is calm and carries a power she's never heard before. "One moment won't hurt. Look." He leans forward and glides his thumbnail over the outer casing of a twig. The motion is gentle, and Viola gapes at the tenderness in his gaze. "Look," he repeats. "There's green underneath."

Sure enough, a hint of verdure peeks out from under the damaged bark. Viola hears the reverence in his voice and shakes her head. *He is completely brainwashed by whatever cult raised him. They should be shut down by the empire, just to stop them from indoctrinating people this way.* A voice pipes up from the depths of her mind. *Isn't that what the empire is doing to me? Shutting me up and silencing me because my choice to become a storyteller threatens the structure of power?*

She spins on her heel and strides off without a backward glance, fighting off the voice of her conscience. Within moments she hears the boy's familiar steps crunching beside her. She's grateful when he maintains the silence. She knows she can't bear any more of his religious zeal, but doesn't want to snap at him either. *It is strange*, she muses. *A few weeks ago, I would not have cared whether he stayed or went his own way, but now—now I have gotten used to his company, strange as it is. I like him, even if he sprouts all that nonsense. Maybe I should try harder to understand him. There is a lot about him that doesn't fit into the picture of the universe I have been taught. Not now—I don't think I have the patience for it today.*

As the silence draws out between them, a soft blanket shared by two companions, Viola's attention is drawn upwards to the azure sky. For the first time in a while, she actually sees the big blue expanse stretching above her with its crimson disc hovering over the horizon while the blazing ball of ivory begins its descent. She notes the varying shades of the canopy, which changes tone from blazing periwinkle to sun-kissed sapphire. *It is beautiful*, she acknowledges to herself but is loath to voice her recognition out loud. *He would probably gloat if I said anything.* She cloaks herself in her grumpy mien, an easy deterrent for continued conversation.

On the horizon, dark clouds hover in the direction they're walking, mimicking the darkness she draws about herself. Time is running out, and she needs a plan. Her destination draws nearer, but how can she keep herself and the boy safe? Mulling over the pattern she has seen in the way she's pursued, Viola begins formulating a strategy.

A few days later, Viola relaxes her feet, sitting on a stool in the cool of the first roadside inn they've frequented since their meeting. She leans her elbows against the rough-hewn wooden table and observes the room with its stone walls and empty tables spread around the area. There are few travellers this time of year, what with the heat and the blight. She knows it makes them vulnerable, more noticeable. One wrong word and evil's beastly minions could be swarming the place within a few short hours.

Through an arch to her left, she hears the innkeeper and his wife bantering to the vibrating sound of a knife chopping vegetables. *Fresh vegetables.* Viola's stomach sings at the thought.

Her skin tingles from her stint scrubbing dust and grime from her arms and face. She revels in the sensation of her pores breathing freely. The rest of her body longs for a good soak to wash away the grime of weeks on the road, but she knows there'll only be enough water for a quick shower and nothing more.

"Here you go." The rotund innkeep sets two bowls on the table with a scrape.

Viola nods and breathes in the fragrance of wholesome vegetable stew. Eyes closed, she savours the anticipation but is jolted back to alertness at the sound of slurping. She sits back, watching the boy who shovels the food into his mouth. In one fell swoop, he's running his finger over the rim of the bowl and licking off the dredges of his stew.

She feels her face twitch into disapproval at the sight of his hands. "You should wash before you eat."

He glances up at her, a sheepish expression in his eyes. "Too hungry," he mutters.

Viola's stomach rumbles, and she turns her attention back to the bowl in front of her. Steam rises off the top, and she inhales the fragrant seasoning again, preparing herself for the burst of flavour. Her spoon dips into the stew. Unlike her apprentice, Viola savours every bite, taking her time. She senses eyes boring into her and bristles. "If you don't have anything better to do, take that bowl to the kitchen and then see if there is a horse or mule we can buy."

His brows arch into crescents of surprise. "Why do we need a pack animal?"

"Because I want one. Now go and see if there is anything suitable."

"Yes, Master."

She breathes a sigh of forbearance and continues eating. *Will it work?* She wonders. *It has to. There is no other way to get into the city and remain unrecognised, and we must stay inconspicuous.* In silence she eats, watching her apprentice's retreating form. Her thoughts snag on his behaviour at mealtimes: shovelling in food with a furtive set to his eyes—as if someone might take it away if he doesn't eat fast enough. *I wish I knew more about him.*

Her stomach satisfied, she makes her way up the stairs to the dormitory above and sits on one of the two pallets. The washstand graces one stone wall of the small square room. There's no window, and the space is gloomy. Viola contemplates her situation, turning over and over in her mind the possibilities and their outcomes.

The boy comes in. "I got a donkey."

She nods. Her thoughts return to him and his desire to tell stories. "Why do you want to be a storyteller?" she asks.

Her curiosity is met with wide eyes. His tongue darts over his lips and he tilts his head to one side. After a moment of introspection, he replies, "I don't know. It's always been there. Every time I listened to the tales they told around the fire on festival nights, it woke something here." He gestures to his heart. "This year, the flame that won't go out became too hard to bear. I had to do something about the longing."

Viola hears the depth of his reverence when he mentions the tales told by his people. *I know nothing of him.* He sidesteps every direct question she asks him about his background or where he comes from. *What people make up his community? Where are they from? How do they survive in this forsaken land? Perhaps this is how I can get him to open up.* "Tell me a tale from your people," she encourages.

She sees his uncharacteristic hesitation, that flash of worry tinged with fear. "You didn't like the last one I started." His voice is laced with hurt.

He inhales, closes his eyes, and Viola observes the signs of a struggle flitting over his features. Wavering, she wonders what she can say to calm him, but before she can formulate anything, he looks at her, a smile gleaming in the depths of his eyes and he begins.

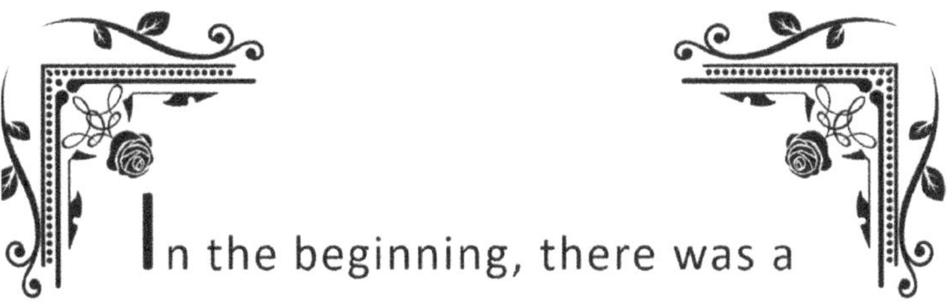

In the beginning, there was a thought. The thought gathered and grew into a ripple of many thoughts. The ripples ebbed and flowed until they found expression in a word. From the first word were born the rays of creation. Thought gave birth to the word. Words brought form and created all that is. The Great Thinker of Things took form through the first word. That consciousness gave expression to creation through the word, the many words that ensued. Thought is the parent of us all, the Mother-Father of all that is. Thought. Word. Creation.

The First Ray, immaterial and energetic, brought forth the powers of creation. It was the tool that birthed the creative powers from the Great Consciousness. Those creators were given more rays to help them in their task. The creative rays, produced by The Great Thought, parent of us all, guided the creative powers through the rays of creation. The Lesser Creators' thoughts and words were shaped by the rays, and together, they brought forth many beautiful things. The creations gathered and grew and became a ripple of many creations; existing in a vast, expansive universe. There was light and sound, but there were no eyes to see, nor ears to hear. All of creation existed in an expansive void.

The Great Thinker of Things thought of life. A word brought forth the Ray of Life, the creative element that the many creators used to bring forth all living things throughout the universe. The beauty of these many creatures brought great joy to the One Who Thinks, but it was not enough. There was something else that tugged at the Great Thought. A new ray was created, a better one, more

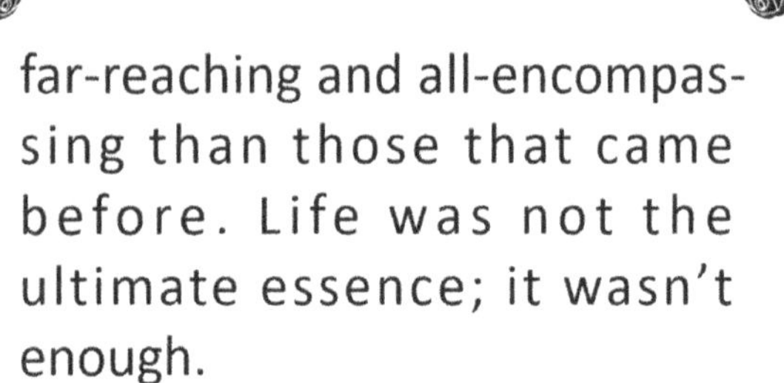

far-reaching and all-encompassing than those that came before. Life was not the ultimate essence; it wasn't enough.

The Great Thinker of Things thought of free will—

Viola sighs. She cradles her head in her hands. The boy trails off, and she glances up, catching a look of uncertainty flitting through his eyes. She shakes her head but feels a resigned smile twitching at the corner of her lips. "Of all the idiotic things," she says. "I knew it was a cult that raised you, but this is too much!" Exasperation lines her voice.

He laughs. "It wasn't how I told the story, but which story I chose?"

"Precisely!" she interjects. "I know I asked for a story from your people, but why do you spout all this religious gobbledygook? Have you not seen the world out there? There is no higher being that will save us all." He bows in her direction, still seated. Viola shakes her head again, "I don't understand you at all."

He shrugs as he bounces to his feet. "It's simple, really. I have faith. All will be well."

"And how can you know that with such certainty?" she retorts, baffled.

"The Great Mother-Father communes with me and told me last night in a dream, *Fear not, all will be well.*" Viola feels consternation burning in her eyes, and disbelief contorting her features. "Do you not believe in something?" he asks, the question tentative.

Viola stands. "No," she replies. "I lost my faith a long time ago, and nothing I have seen since has indicated the workings of a higher being. God does not exist. It is a figment of our imaginations, a false hope to keep the common people placid and exploitable."

She ends the discussion by bedding down and rolling over on her pallet. She stretches her aching muscles, tired from the ordeal of travel. A dull ache in her right knee makes itself known while her thoughts linger on the tale he shared. She's never heard a creation myth like that one. Most peoples speak of powerful dragons breathing fire and air to create the many worlds. At the heart of the empire, no one believes in gods anymore. They've taken up that mantle in their hubris, claiming descent from the gods, and hence, divine right to rule. Time passes before her breaths slow and she drifts into welcoming darkness.

Chapter Five

The boy trots along beside the donkey. He stretches out to touch its fuzzy neck, which twitches in response to the contact. The fur tickles his fingers. Long ears swivel in his direction, then turn forward as the boy smiles to himself. The animal plods at a steady pace, sure-footed and dependable. He's happy to have another living creature for company. It reminds him of his days tending sheep, those few moments of tranquillity and happiness that he misses from the time before he left on this adventure.

White fabric flutters into his vision and draws his gaze downwards. He scratches his head as he considers the outfit Viola insisted he put on a few hours earlier. White shirt and trousers are bound about his waist with a thick cord, and a separate piece of white material is draped over his head, held in place by a textile roll. It constricts him, and he wiggles his scalp to alleviate the discomfort. A light breeze tugs at the head-covering, and it buffets his arms. All in all, it's oddly fun, but irritating because it's unfamiliar.

"Why are we dressing up as Bedouins?" he asks.

Viola glares at him, and he sighs. She's less than forthcoming with information about this sudden change in dress. She wears a similar outfit, and the head covering billowing around her makes her look like she's floating as she walks.

His arm is pulled back by a gentle tug on the rope he holds. He responds by jerking it to his side, encouraging the pack animal to keep up the pace. Then he smiles because having the animal as an extra companion is worth all the oddities accompanying this stage of his journey. He ponders Viola's behaviour—travelling off the beaten track, not announcing that she's a storyteller when they stayed at the inn, insisting on this disguise now. *She's hiding something*, he thinks. Then he shrugs. *I also have secrets. She'll tell me if it's any of my business.*

His gaze wanders over the landscape, and then he wishes it hadn't. Everything the light touches is corrupted by blight. The sand has an indigo tinge to it, and most plants are barely managing to hold onto life, their leaves luminous with unnatural shades of green and yellow. Blackened stalks litter the empty spaces between the few hardy plants. Their journey keeps taking them deeper into contaminated country and ever closer to the mountains on the horizon.

They often pass run-down towns. Some are even abandoned, lifeless husks where people used to thrive. The few villagers remaining in these places are always old and infirm—walking skeletons. The boy's heart constricts at the sight of these spectres. *How can this suffering be acceptable?* His consternation is ignored, as are his questions. He has the presence of mind, however, not to push the subject with his travelling companion. His skills of observation serve him well. He sees the storm-cloud brewing within Viola's eyes, he hears her heavy sighs and dark mutterings, he senses the weight she, too, bears from the suffering she sees. Conversations with her have dwindled to the bare bones of communication. They don't talk about anything beyond food and sleep.

He also understands the futility of the task his people perform. With only fifty members in their community and the time required for them to achieve their work, it's impossible to keep up with the blight. There's too much of it, too much destruction; human neglect and greed will bring everything to crumbling dust. He feels despair settle about his shoulders. It's a cumbersome mantle that drags at his feet, weight pulling him towards the ground.

Since leaving the inn where they bought the donkey, they spend their nights in abandoned homes—half-caved-in lean-tos of rotting planks, crumbled ruins which were once brick buildings. There are no welcoming inns at regular intervals. Days pass without sight of potable water; the riverbed is dry, coated in mauve crystals, tinged in lime. Even most wells in the towns are dry—or worse, contaminated. Viola has stopped recounting new tales every night. Their rhythm from before the incident with the meerkats is long forgotten. She withdraws into herself. The boy wonders about her reticence but dares not ask for the lightning he fears within her thunder-cloud demeanour.

"We are nearing the city," Viola says, tugging at the pack animal's rope in an attempt to make it hurry.

The boy is relieved. He tips his bottle and licks the last drop from the rim. He's also excited. What wonders might the city hold? He's only ever heard of such mythical places; he's never seen one with his own eyes. His people speak of cities as demonic places where evil reigns, but they must be mistaken. *Surely, people wouldn't move there from the Outlands if the city is as noxious as they claim,* he thinks.

The next day begins with a scratching sensation at the back of his throat and ominous clouds on the horizon. As time passes, a roiling black nebula obscures both suns, bringing an unnatural twilight with it. The wind sweeps the sulphurous stench of industry to his nose, which wrinkles in disgust.

Towering jagged rocks emerge on a plateau in the

distance, rising above a flat surface. All else is concealed by the overhanging clouds and a perplexing haze that sweeps over the rock-like spires—as though an artist has wiped a damp sponge over a painting. They draw nearer, and the boy's awareness shifts. The towers aren't rocks at all; they're buildings—mountains of square cubes fading into each other in a mixture of grey, brown and black, all perched atop a sheer rock wall beyond which lies an unidentifiable surface.

The roiling purple mass of congealed industrial brew that belches forth from interminable chimney stacks obscures everything and rains down a drizzle of dusty ash, coating all it touches in a layer of mulberry dust. The city-grime accumulates on his skin, mixing with his sweat and running in rivulets down the corners of his eyes and mouth. Viola coughs and spits a lump of dark phlegm onto the ground. He shudders.

Through the haze, the boy finally makes out some details of the gigantic wall. He can see that it spans a valley to the west of the city. Miles and miles of steep, smooth concrete stretch as far as the eye can see, joining the cliff face where the city perches. Viola leads the way towards it, and his mind fills in the gap in his knowledge with *dam wall*. Her face is grim. He follows, tugging the donkey behind him.

Hours pass before the concrete structure towers above them, blotting out everything except the ominous clouds. The boy and the animal trot on after Viola, who comes to a halt at a shadowy building. It's a squat rectangle huddling in the obscurity cast by the wall behind and the clouds above. A cavernous square hole breaks the building's monotonous exterior.

"Stay here with the donkey," Viola commands before striding inside.

The boy feels tension rolling off her and rippling under his skin. He doesn't know what this place is. His mind doesn't offer him a special name to go with it. For once, his word-brain is silent. The absence only makes uncertainty gnaw harder at his bowels. What is going on?

Viola reappears, the pale fabric billowing out behind her in a gust of air. She's followed by a short man dressed in imperial white. His pristine jacket strains over a large belly in its attempt to reach his hips. A high collar presses its way into his wobbling jowls as he leans forward to inspect the donkey. In his pudgy hands, he holds a sleek, black device that shimmers dully in the half-light of the afternoon. What strikes the boy most, though, is the man's clean-shaven cheeks. All the men in his village display their beards with pride, the symbol of their masculinity. This man without facial hair seems wrong, almost unnatural.

The boy glances between Viola and the man, who studies the apparatus in his hands, mutters something, then peeks into Viola's backpack, slung across the donkey like a saddlebag. "Personal effects," he mumbles.

The storyteller has a fist clenched. Her breathing is shallow, her eyes never leaving the man's fingers as they dance over his device. The donkey stamps, drawing the boy's attention and in that moment, he sees a shimmer around his master. Viola, the person he knows and has travelled with for weeks, shifts into the background and instead, he sees a man with a thick beard and dark, weather-beaten skin.

Startled, he looks at her again, and Viola's true form replaces the mirage. *What's going on?* He can't put his finger on it, but his writhing innards tell him something odd is afoot. He glances away, and out of the corner of his eye, he sees the shift happen again. When he's not looking at her, she appears to be a man, a Bedouin who's trudged the Mshrali dust bowl his whole life.

"All clear," the official intones, dismissing them with a twitch of his finger. "Welcome to Ilwych and report to the tax authority if you wish to conduct business."

"Thank you, sir," Viola replies, her voice rumbling in an unnatural baritone. "Have a nice day." She strides off, leaving the gaping boy to stare at her back until she snaps over her shoulder, "Come along, boy!"

He trots to catch up with her, but she doesn't wait. A thousand questions pour through his mind, and he has to still the confusion. Each problem swells to the surface, and he releases it, knowing this is another of those things she won't explain. *She doesn't trust me with her secrets, and why would she? I'm just a boy who forced myself on her with my petition. She probably sees me as a burden.*

That's not true; the voice of his conscience is decisive. *She's been accommodating, helpful and shows signs of truly caring. It's just that her burdens are heavy, and she holds them close. I don't think she's used to sharing them.*

They reach the wall, and he looks up, following the vertical slice to where it disappears from view in the gloom of the clouds. Viola marches up a set of stairs along the side of the barrier. She doesn't stop, nor does she look back. The donkey baulks at the bottom of the staircase. Patient and soothing, the boy coaxes the creature forwards, step by agonising step up a narrow ramp beside the stairs. After an interminable battle of wills, they reach the top, his ears ringing from the donkey's braying.

As he stops to catch his breath, feeling the smog particles permeate his lungs, the boy's gaze falls upon the vista beyond the wall: water, midnight blue in the shadowy half-light. The unruffled expanse stretches all the way to the mountains, which loom much closer than he realised. His mouth is dry; his tongue is a lump of sandpaper grating against his cheeks and teeth.

"Come along!" Viola exclaims.

She's already at the door of a square building that

overlooks the great dam. A sign hangs above the arched doorway which is screened by a string of beads and bells. The picture on the sign is so faded that he can't make it out, but he imagines it indicates that the building is an inn. Behind the smooth grey cube of the inn, the city sprawls with its dark blocks—stacks of squares and rectangles climbing into the dark sky.

The boy draws in a deep breath to still his hammering heart and soothe the way his stomach clenches. This is all so different from the flat open landscape he's accustomed to. He glances one last time at the smooth liquid behind him, as though hoping the presence of so much water will calm him. It doesn't. His eye catches sight of whorls of violet that taint the surface—purple streaked with virulent pink. He shivers and trots off to Viola's side, tugging at his animal companion who is more than willing to keep up with them.

Chapter Six

Apprehension gnaws at Viola. She paces the small room she's been given to share with her apprentice. She ignores the wooden panelling on the walls, focusing all her attention on the worn floor that's seen better days. Three steps, turn, and back again. Every so often she pauses, struck by a thought but then shakes her head and resumes wearing a path into the wood under her feet. Worry gathers like a thundercloud above her head. Her shoulders sag with the weight of her misgivings. What to do?

A thought strikes and she lifts her gaze from the floor. She heads over to her backpack, rummages through it and pulls out a small pouch. Then her face falls. *It is not enough. It is not going to work. I am going to have to leave him behind.* In response to that thought, her gut wrenches in a hard twist. *There is no way*, she decides. *I must accept it and move on. All I can do is provide him as many tools as possible before that moment is upon us.*

Viola is out of the door in the blink of an eye and rushes down the stairs. Following a hallway, she comes out into a peristyle. Tall columns hold up a slanting roof, allowing passage around the central open area, which is filled with green and the tinkling of water. The peacefulness of the place captivates her. She takes a deep breath, revelling in how clean the air is, and absorbs the stillness, calming her pounding heart.

She glances around her. Marble benches line the outer walls, which are shielded by the roof. The light filtering through the clouds above brightens the green centre with its fountain, drawing the eye to this patch of life at the heart of all the solid brick-and-cement death of the city. Viola's gaze falls on a figure sitting with its back to a raised wall that encloses the central pool of water. Recognising her travelling companion, she stops to study him.

The boy's eyes are closed. His head rests on the lip of the stone wall; his face is turned towards the brightness that pushes its way through the thick purple mass blanketing the whole city. Although there's no direct sunlight, he looks peaceful. The knot returns to her stomach. Can she go through with what she must do? *This is exactly why I should not have agreed to take him on as an apprentice in the first place. These kinds of attachment are what will get me, or both of us killed. I have to be strong. I made the mistake of getting connected, allowing his bright smile and cheerful nature to tug at my heart. My loneliness drove me to the desire for company, but it will all come to dust and pain.*

She sighs, and his eyes fly open at the sound. Viola wants to step back; she's in no mood to be talking to him. Then she remembers what she came to say. She returns her attention to the boy but pauses again when she notices that he's studying her. Despite herself, her mouth draws into a thin line. *Does he always have to do that? Can he not look past me like everyone else does?* The look he sends her somehow speaks to her soul and stirs the dissatisfaction, which for years, she's kept under a tight lid. She doesn't want to think about all the things she longed for, everything she gave up, just to end up here.

Viola shifts uncomfortably, then clears her throat. "It is time for the next stage of your training. You know a selection of tales; now you need to learn to perform them."

He comes to his feet in one smooth motion. Jealousy sends a twitch through her jaw. Viola can't remember a time when she could move like that and her knee aches in acknowledgement of the thought. He looks at her expectantly, and she banishes her dark thoughts.

"It is time to test you out in public. Let us see if you can engage passers-by near the market."

His face glows like a beacon. Another guilt-wrenched spasm goes through her. *How can I disappoint him so?* The firm voice of her reason responds with unwavering certainty. *It has to be this way. I cannot keep him with me. That would be impossible.*

She whirls and leads the way out of the inn and down the cobbled street. It's lined with dilapidated concrete structures that have seen better days. Some buildings have rounded piles of soot weighing down their flat roofs and Viola wonders how long they've been abandoned. Even though with the help of machines, the streets are swept daily, grime covers everything, giving off a dark purple hue on all open surfaces.

Viola observes the cloud-cover above them. It resonates with the gloom she feels within. Why does everything always have to be so hard? Then she banishes despair by throwing herself into the task at hand.

They come out onto a large market square covered over with a tarpaulin roof. The half-light of the market is filled with different-sized stalls and a stew of odours. The smell of blood is heavy in the air because they enter the area near the butcher-stalls. There's a cacophony of merchants calling their wares, haggling, and the sounds of live animals trussed up and ready for slaughter. The level of noise is overwhelming, and Viola steers her apprentice through the bustling throng to another of the streets adjoining the square. She gives the boy instructions but even while she's talking, she wonders if it will be of any help to him.

He sets himself up at the edge of the market and Viola stays a little distance away to observe, but not to interfere. This is his test, and he must show whether he can handle the pressure. She sees him glance up into the gloom above, then he squares his shoulders and lurches into *The Destitute Countess*, one of the tales she taught him on their way to the city.

Within moments, she ceases to focus on his words. A shimmer appears around him as he becomes immersed in the tale he weaves. As he glows brighter and brighter, she realises that the hint of rainbow lights she saw playing about him when he told her his very first tale was nothing compared to his true power. It takes all her might to contain the undulations of refracted light—she knows this ability of his will draw unwanted attention, and she must avoid that at all costs, but she also owes him. She feels responsible for him in a way. *I cannot just abandon him on the street. Especially not here in Ilwych; he will never survive. I have to provide him with the tools to make a living out here.*

While Viola combats the strength of his light, which strains to break free from her attempts to suppress it, the boy begins to draw a crowd. The more people gather to listen, the more others notice him standing there. The crowd swells with every passing minute, and as his final word echoes into silence, there are close to a hundred bystanders.

Jubilation erupts, and people press forward to congratulate him, asking him where he'll be performing next. Many press small coins into his hand, thanking him for the upliftment. When the throng disperses, Viola sees his eyes glistening in a mixture of awe, shock, and delight. She rejoins him, claps him on the shoulder and nods. Her own words have dried up. Now, worry has thinned her blood, making it race faster than ever. *I cannot leave him, even though I must. What am I going to do now?*

With the last remnant of her willpower, she pulls herself together and forces words out of her mouth. She talks about intonation, posture and getting even closer to the people with inflexion. She sees a flicker dash through his deep brown eyes but ignores the reproach that rears its head within her. He must learn, and as much as possible in a short while. *There is no time for pride.*

They reach the inn once more, and Viola leaves him to rest, saying, "This was a very promising start. I will see whether there are any opportunities at a tavern. You go and rest, and I shall make the arrangements."

She watches him take the stairs to the upper floor of the building. His feet tread lightly. Her memory floods with the image of his brightness, the way his eyes sparkle when he tells a story, and the set of his shoulders as he walks, the setting sun reaching beneath the cloud and lighting the horizon behind him. *How do I see to his success without drawing too much attention?* She knows it's a fine line she treads. *He is my apprentice.* It's her duty to see him learn what he must to succeed, but there's also his life to think about.

Turning, she brushes away her conundrum. She'll have to find a way. That's the only option left to her.

Later that evening, weary from all the places she's been and people she's talked to, Viola returns to the inn. On her way there, she crosses the now deserted marketplace. She stops. There's something unusual about the vast, open expanse. She glances about the murky space and understanding hits her. There's no litter here. Everything is clean and neat, nothing at all like a marketplace is commonly left after a long day of bartering in the heat. Not even traces of blood can be seen on the flagstones, which glisten in the half-light. Even the grey-purple dust that covers all surfaces in this city is gone, revealing beige sandstone and grey cement.

The oddity is striking. She knows this place. The streets are only ever scrubbed like this before festival days, or for the visit of an important imperial official. Aware that neither of these scenarios is imminent, she wonders what might have occurred here. She takes a detour, exploring this strange phenomenon and notices that the further she gets away from the marketplace, the dirtier the street becomes. Changing direction, she approaches the market square along a different route and finds that the same applies. Accumulated grime dwindles as she approaches the market.

How can this be? The people of this city are notorious for their disregard for cleanliness. It is something one can expect of those accustomed to living year in and year out in a cloud of malignant purple. At a loss, Viola scratches her head and then continues on her way. *An intriguing little mystery to distract me, but cleanliness in this city is not worth wasting time on. It is late, and I had better get back.*

As she continues her trajectory, another thought filters to the surface. *If he is, by some miracle, affecting the people in this way, then I must bind his powers to him for it will only draw attention. I must be more alert and do what I can to keep him safe.*

Chapter Seven

The boy watches Viola; with each passing day, she becomes more agitated. Although he wonders why, he doesn't feel it's his place to ask her such a pointed question. He isn't used to inquiring about people. His past has honed him to observe and then to fill in the blanks with reasonable calculation. However, her secretiveness and heightened irritability are becoming more and more noticeable. He feels his tension increase as the days pass. *Something is happening.*

Viola is out. He doesn't know where she is or what she plans. Not knowing what he should do under the circumstances weighs upon him. A thought flits across his mind, and he kneels in their shared room to ask his god for guidance.

"Great Mother-Father," he murmurs. "You brought

me here and allowed me to meet the Master Storyteller. What can I do to help? How can I serve?"

He waits in silence, but no answer comes. Stillness envelops him.

When Viola doesn't return in the late afternoon, he goes back to the garden bordered by the peristyle. He sits in his favourite place beside the pool, and at length, he drifts into a fitful sleep.

The city glows in sunlight; the purple shadows cast by clouds are a distant memory of days gone by. The dam sparkles crystalline perfection, and he sees fish ripple under the surface. Streets gleam, their dusty, grimy past long forgotten. People stop to talk to each other, helping one another. Trees grow beside the roads, casting shade over the walkways. Plants dangle tendrils from window sills, and everywhere he looks, bright colours dazzle the eye. Birds sweep and whirl in the sky, their songs mingling on the breeze.

His eyes fly open. He stares up at the plum-coloured smoke swirling above the rectangle defined by the slanting roof. *So much is possible. I know that what I saw in that vision can be done, but how?* He pauses, feeling the walls of his mind encase him. *How,* he repeats, as those walls turn to iron. He visualises what the word does to his thoughts. *That question traps me in the current situation. It doesn't serve me or what I wish to achieve.*

What part can I play? In their eyes, I'm just a youth from an uncultured backwater. What can I do to make the beauty I see a reality for all to experience? His rational mind overrides the consideration. *It's impossible. What can humble little me do? I'm nothing.*

The reply flashes through to the surface of his conscious mind, bright and true. *I am a child of the Great Parent. The Mother-Father watches over me. As long as I adhere to the ordinances, I'll always find my way.*

He comes to his feet and paces a square around the artificial pool at the centre of the garden sanctuary. The columns of the peristyle, solid tree trunks of marble, keep him company—the larger square to his smaller one. The shrubs, the water, the image of trees beyond his experience of such plants—for the trees he knows are small and stunted by the heat of his home—all of it comes together in a sweeping image of peacefulness, and he knows he can trust in the vision. *This is what matters. I don't need to know how I'll achieve it, but I do know it's possible.*

Beyond the row of columns, movement at the doorway draws his gaze. He sees Viola. She wears simple trousers and a shirt. Nothing flamboyant. Nothing to mark her trade. Her look is forgettable, and he wonders about the reasons behind that. From the little he knows of her, she seems most comfortable in the bright cloak with the big hat, as he saw her the evening they met. Nostalgia strikes. *How long?* he muses. *How many weeks have we travelled together and yet I know almost nothing about her?*

His eyes capture hers. Something flickers in the depths of those violet pools. *Was that guilt?* He brushes it off, taking in other details instead, as though focusing on trifles could distract the truth he senses in his heart. Her dark hair is cut shorter than he's seen it before; it doesn't play about her ears anymore. Her hands fiddle with a scrap of paper. She looks down at her fingers, then flickers back to his eyes. *Nervousness? Fear?*

Viola clears her throat, "You are expected at the Beacon Tavern, down the road, tomorrow at second sundown."

Before the words settle into his understanding, she spins and marches off. The boy feels his face scrunch up. *Something is wrong; that isn't the way the Master usually is.* Since they reached the city, his short-tempered, irascible travelling companion has become increasingly preoccupied and apprehensive.

He goes over the details of the encounter again and considers other oddities from recent days. *She's leaving.* The thought blazes through his mind, freezing his heart in the surprising brightness. His first thought: *How could she?* Is pushed aside by another, even before it's fully formed. *Of course; she's leaving. She's on the run from something, and they clearly won't stop. She's terrified of whoever is after her, and that means they must have power.*

His heart speeds up at the memory of the drone, sweeping over the scrub searching—for her. He realises he knew it even on that first day. At some intuitive level, he'd understood what was at stake, but he'd kept the knowledge aside so he wouldn't think about it.

Understanding is followed by an accusation. *She used me! I was the perfect cover, changing her habits and making them overlook us because they were looking for one lone traveller.* The idea that he's been used is etched with a feeling of betrayal. It takes a moment before compassion pushes through, crashing in to smooth over his resentment. *Yes, perhaps she used me and will leave, but she's also seeing to it that I won't starve. She's made sure to teach me what I need to know, and even at this moment, she is showing me my path by preparing me for the future. She's my Master, and she embraced that role. I have to help her.*

Air pours into his lungs. Sweet substance of life. Purpose burns strong and unwavering in the core of his being. It lights him up and motivates him to excel, so the work she's found him might also benefit her. *She must need money*, he muses. *She can't travel without it, and there wasn't much left when we got here. She paid for me—is paying for me. It's time I return that gift and lighten her load.*

That night, he lies awake a long time, listening to Viola's breathing, envisioning his success at the Beacon Tavern. He wonders which story to tell—ponders what is fitting for the place and circumstance of his engagement. When the answer comes to him, he smiles broadly. It resonates with his vision from earlier that afternoon. The realisation that he can do it all—achieve his desire to help Viola, fulfil his dream of becoming a storyteller, and also take a firm step towards seeing this befouled city become a vibrant place of life—rides at the forefront of sleep, which sweeps over him moments later and brings him to the dark world of tranquillity and rest.

The next day, the boy wakes with electric sparks of excitement coursing through him. Time passes at a leisurely pace. Throughout the day, all he can think about is his official debut as a storyteller. He revels in his luck at stumbling across Viola, for she has proven herself to be the most fitting teacher. In a few short weeks, she's coached him to become a viable storyteller, and the knowledge sends a flurry of butterflies through his being.

His excitement is tempered somewhat by concern. Viola is absent for most of the day, and when she does return in the late afternoon, the first sun is grazing the horizon and the second is ready to descend past the flat expanse beyond the city. He observes, by the set of her jaw and the dullness in her eyes, that she's afraid. Her fear fans his determination and increases his desire to succeed, and in so doing, help her.

Instead of asking her pointed questions about the cause of her fear, he bows his head in acknowledgement and murmurs, "Thank you, Master, for granting me this opportunity. I'll be sure to make you proud at the Beacon Tavern."

Distracted, Viola mutters a soft, "Yes, yes." Then she heads upstairs.

He takes a deep breath, invokes a blessing from his deity, and sets off down the road. His stomach writhes in apprehension, but he knows this is the good fear that will allow him to perform at his very best. His eyes scan the buildings on either side of the street. When he catches sight of the second disk turning luminous orange, he increases his pace. *Don't want to be late.* His agitation has him casting about, and he almost misses the faded sign of a strange tower that hangs from the eaves.

The boy frowns at the image on the sign. The construction seems out of place in this city at the edge of a desert. The word *lighthouse* does flit through his mind, but he suppresses the novel concept, pushing it aside. *Must focus.*

He's about to step through the doors when a voice calls out behind him, "Wait!"

Turning around, he sees Viola sprint up to his side. She bends over double, wheezing to catch her breath. He notices she favours her left leg and offers her a hand to support her, but she waves him off. “You go in and ask for Lorian. I shall be watching.”

Chapter Eight

Viola hangs back in the darkness. She observes the patrons in the tavern. They're burly men coated in city-grime, their brows heavy with a long day's work. Their eyes are hard, revealing souls accustomed to toiling in hazardous conditions, now softening in the glow of an evening drink and some coveted tobacco before heading back to their barracks for bed. *Miners. A very hard life. I wonder whether he can charm them.*

The boy steps up onto a raised platform in one corner of the room where lamps surround him with a golden glow. He's thin but doesn't have the lost waif look he had before. His eyes glitter with excitement and nerves as he glances into the hazy gloom of the tavern. His bow is met with a series of guffaws and rude comments.

"Change his diaper and send him home to his mommy! We want a real fabler, not some whelp!"

"Barkeep, get the half-pint a cup of milk and bring out the cookies."

Laughter follows and Viola bristles but keeps her own counsel. Her eyes fix on the boy as he launches into his tale without even glancing at the group of disparaging commentators. Within moments the chatter of many conversations stills. Even the sounds from the bar—clinking glasses, the tinkle of coins and the bubbling pot on the hob—seem to cease. Silence fills the room.

Viola smiles. *He has got this right. Such a bright and promising apprentice.* She shuts off the lingering feeling of guilt at her imminent departure and the fact that he'll lose out on the full training he should receive. Is she failing him?

Colours begin to dance about the boy, and she focuses her attention on weaving a net around them, forcing them within and reducing that inner light to a mere flicker. The work keeps her mind away from idle musings that usually settle in a dark cloud about her shoulders. When he finishes, Viola feels his eyes bore into her. She bows her head, acknowledging him, and even smiles. *He has done well*, she thinks as she ties off her binding with a flick of the wrist. *Why did I not think to tether his powers before this? It is an excellent way to keep him out of harm's way, and it should hide them for a few years.* She wishes she knew what it meant, though. She brushes off the thought. She doesn't have time for doubts; she has to go, and he can't come with her. This is one way to keep him safe without him being by her side.

That night, Viola sleeps better than she has in a long time. The fear and uncertainty gnawing in her stomach release their hold—if only for one night—and she finds rest. The following morning at breakfast, the boy, her apprentice, pushes a pouch across the table. Viola looks at it, then glances at him. He smiles but doesn't say anything.

Viola chooses to ignore the offering, so he shifts it towards her more decisively and says, "You paid for my lodging here. It's only right you see some of that returned."

His kindness overwhelms her. *He is too good. He will be ruined if I leave him, as I must.* Anger at the injustice of the situation burns within her, brushing aside her sense of gratitude. Tears prick behind her eyeballs, and Viola clenches her fist in an attempt to force them into submission. The overwhelming mixture of conflicting emotions brings her to her feet.

Realising how ungracious she appears, Viola closes her fingers around the pouch and in the same instant meets his gaze. She hopes he can read her gratitude there because she knows her voice will crack if she tries to speak. Then, in her habit of obscuring her emotions, she pulls a mantle of indifference about her and stalks off, leaving in her wake a half-finished plate and a confused boy.

Viola paces back and forth in the room. Things are not working out as she needs them to and anxiety claws at her. Back and forth she goes in a whirlwind of tension. She sees what she needs within her grasp, and yet, it's slipping through her fingers. *I just don't have enough.* If she can't get one decent engagement, the opportunity will slide from her grasp and then the game will be over.

For a split second, she contemplates giving up. Then her simmering anger balls its fists and riles, *Never!* No, she knows she won't give up. She has to keep fighting. She stops her pacing, and her sigh reverberates into her toes, *I am so tired of it all.* She racks her brain once more. *How to do it?* Her mind is a barren desert. No ideas come to her, and she gnashes her teeth in frustration.

A shuffling sound at the doorway startles Viola from her contemplation. Heart leaping into her throat, she spins around, and her gaze locks with the familiar, deep brown eyes. Her apprentice's compassion and worry pour into her, overwhelming her. She glances away, breaking the connection if only to keep a semblance of control.

"Master," he ventures. "Is there any way I can help?"

"No." Her reaction is automatic, visceral and the result of many long years' practise and the need to rely on herself. Her fist clenches and she keeps her back turned to him.

"We both know that isn't true." His words are soft but carry an unwavering certainty. "What is it you wish for, Master?"

His words open a crack in the seawall she's spent years constructing. In spite of herself, her words spill forth. "I need one sizeable event. I need to make a lot of cash in a single night." She feels the entire ocean of the worries she's been holding at bay, come crashing through, reducing her barrier to rubble. "What is the point in striving? It is hopeless. I am stuck in this forsaken back-water, and they will get me here, cornered." She gestures at the corner of the room for emphasis, "I will be butchered like the last shaggy bear of Harland after hounds tormented it, nipping at its legs and keeping it at bay." One hand slashes symbolically across the other wrist as she continues, "I might as well end it all and foil their plans for me. There will not be a victory parade on my account. At least I can choose where and how I shall die."

She stops, her frustrated tirade engulfed by the boy's expression. The sadness in his eyes halts everything. All thought, all emotion—all of it is swallowed by the chasm of his despair.

He takes a deep breath. "And how will that change anything?"

Viola hears the effort it takes for him to keep his voice steady. She's struck by his words. They reach her in a way she's never experienced before. There's something profound about how they plough into her, melting away all her practised defences and striking her heart, releasing the pent-up ache she's held there.

"What meaning could there possibly be for such an action?" His tone is soft, the type of comforter she's been avoiding all these years. She sees the pit of suffering simmering beneath his gaze and understanding shocks its way through her in a tingling strike. *I am not alone. My suffering might be my own, but we all suffer in one way or another. It is what I do with what I have that should count, that could make a difference.*

The boy goes on, "What would happen to everything you've done so far?"

Again, his words are a resonant gong in her soul. Viola swallows hard against the brick that appears to have lodged in her chest cavity. "It would all disappear," she murmurs.

"Yes. It would become utterly meaningless. Your experiences, everything you've ever done, what you've suffered and what you achieved despite the suffering—it will all be lost, and you, Viola Alerion, Master of Words, greatest storyteller to grace this empire, you will be forgotten. What possible good could come of such loss?"

She's silent. She has no words to respond with. Her apprentice soldiers on, a determined crease forming between his eyebrows. "I know the Mother-Father would never condone such waste. You have tried to respond to your purpose, and you have endured, swimming against the stream, fighting to keep going. Would you really squander it all? Could you let it all be for nothing?"

She bites down on her lower lip. The motion and the pain are enough to patch up the breach in her defences, and she wills the threatening torrent back into comparative calm.

He shifts, the soft rustle of fabric on wood. There's silence, and she glances around to find him sitting cross-legged on the floor, eyes closed. After a moment, he looks up at her, fierce brightness shining in his eyes. "You say you need a lot of money. What haven't you tried yet, Master?"

Viola senses her eyebrows pull together into a sharp V. *What does he mean? I have tried everything!* She's about to burst forth in a tirade when a thought strikes. She stops. Revelation hits her with such force it petrifies all else. She's enveloped in stillness. There's only one thing she can do. A smile creeps over her lips. She has the sharpest arrow to nock to her bow, and she knows this cannot fail.

She's out of the door and down the hallway before

realising that she forgot to thank the boy. A single-minded objective drives her forward, crushing all other thoughts in its way.

Viola returns after dark. Her heart is light. It is the first time in years that she feels the freedom of achieving something seemingly impossible in one fell swoop. Buoyed by high spirits, she leaps up the stairs and steps into the room she shares with her apprentice. Then she stops, her triumphant words falling into silence.

The boy kneels on the hard floorboards. His copper arms are stretched out above his head, his angular face tilted heavenwards. She hears the torrent of words but understands nothing. He speaks in his own tongue; one she never even knew existed before she met him. Every day she has watched him perform his prayers, and each time she's been dumbfounded by the gratitude she hears in his voice. *How can he be so grateful when he has lived through so much hardship?* His unwavering belief disturbs her.

Viola is no newcomer to religious thought; her early education included a listing of all the belief-systems throughout the Haldrian Empire, but never once has she trusted in any of it. Most certainly not with the deep inner conviction displayed by this boy—this apprentice she saddled herself with. He's a mystery to her. She recalls a few times he failed to perform the daily prayer—all of them since they arrived in the city. *Perhaps his faith is being shaken by all of this. I wonder what he thinks of human life, the empire and the rest of it.* Then she remembers their conversation about life that burgeons under the surface, of goodness and choices, and she shakes her head.

The boy finishes, and Viola takes the final step into the room. He beams up at her, his teeth a row of dazzling pearls between thin brown lips, his eyes a contrast of smouldering coals, and she bites back the interrogation waiting to burst forth.

This is not the time.

But if not now, then when? another voice retorts from within. *You will soon part ways with him, so the time for it is now.* She smiles at him and searches for a kind way to begin the conversation she keeps putting off.

"What do you ask for when you pray?"

He tilts his head, an action she has learned to associate with thinking. She can't make out what, but after a brief pause, he replies, "I don't ask for anything. Prayer is for gratitude and conversation. I thank the Mother-Father for all the nice things that come to pass every day."

"How, in all this human affliction, do you find anything to be grateful for?"

A smile spreads over his thin face, "I have food in my

belly, a roof over my head, and a teacher who enlightens me every day. How could I not be grateful for such blessings?"

"And what does this Mother-Father of yours have to say about all the suffering?"

"We all make our choices. Everyone chooses their path."

"So how will anything change?" she retorts, anger rising.

"If you don't believe that you can do something today to make tomorrow better, then you have lost your right to judge. Each one of us must play our part. We can choose to change ourselves and what we do. We can't change others, only guide them to see their potential."

The answer is so direct, so clear and unwavering, that Viola feels as if she's been slapped. She frowns, but before she can think of a response, he continues. "You criticise religion. From the way you talk, I see you think belief in a higher being robs people of their will. You act as though it makes them weak and easy to manipulate. Is that not what you do with your tales? Do you not feed the people what they want to hear, what they need to remain steadfast and content with their lot in life? Do you not distract them with pretty tales of heroic deeds in faraway lands, drawing their attention away from the suffering they live—which they cause themselves? How are you any different from the preacher I've seen haranguing people from the steps of the temple?"

Viola takes a step back. For the first time in her life, she struggles to find words. Even her thoughts are in turmoil. She grasps at one concept and the words that go with it, but it slips through her fingers, the phrases catching in her throat. The boy looks up at her and she realises he has filled out, and possibly even grown a little taller. His gaze is now only a little lower than her own. Determination and conviction shimmer in his dark eyes. An aura of steadfastness settles over him. He's so compelling that her gaze remains captivated.

The boy takes a deep breath, steadies his words and continues, "The Mother-Father taught me that belief is not the same as religion. I can see that what I live is different from what you see. You know religion: the preacher who tells people what to believe, the scriptures that prescribe how you should be. Belief may come from there, but that's not the only way. Belief is within you, not anyone else. You cannot be taught belief; it has to grow inside your heart. You reject religion, but what of belief? Have you truly allowed it to die too?" He pauses to catch his breath, and Viola sees him waver. Will he continue or not?

"Master, I see the inequality, the suffering, and the contamination trouble you. All of it affects you. It upsets me too. You know right from wrong; there's a moral system within you. I see it every time you mutter about the evils of the empire. But remember, that moral system is encoded in religion. We learn it from our parents, our teachers, and the priests. They're the guiding principles in my religion, and probably also in the one you left behind. Those who abandon the moral code are the ones who truly lose their way. But I've seen that look come over you. You do care—deeply. And that means you must believe in something—otherwise, you'd be lost, and I would never have wished to be your apprentice."

Viola shakes herself, as though waking from a dream and in that moment of clarity stops to consider the strength of this boy's language. *How does he know such words?* It's a mystery she files away for later because he's looking at her, waiting for an answer. "No, boy. There's nothing. I believe only that death will come to all of us."

"I suppose recognising that you're alive is a good start," the boy says, a cheeky gleam sparking in his eyes. Viola scowls, but before she can say anything, he continues, "I believe that you work for good. You do wish to end the suffering you encounter. I'm certain you will be able to see the choices you make and will choose good, not evil. You will do your part to end suffering and destruction, for your moral compass is strong, even if you haven't listened to it much in recent times."

"Believe what you wish," Viola retorts with a wave of her hand. "I have witnessed the festering maggot-riddled entity that is human society. We are nothing but a pestilence, a disease, spreading from planet to planet, despoiling everything we touch. There is no point to it, unless of course, we are the natural course of planetary life: organisms that control the power and effects of other life forms so some planets might die and others survive. Everything is death. We—human beings—are meaningless."

"There's good and there's evil," he says, "just as there's life and there's death—so we can learn to know the difference. These two aspects exist in us and through us. They give us the opportunity to choose what is right. Why is this so hard to understand? We each get to pick which path we want to follow. We all have good and evil living inside us. Our choices are what make life meaningful. Yes, there's destruction and death, but there's also so much light and life. There are people who do the right thing, and there are people like you, who hurt for all that's wrong in this universe. It would be easy to achieve change if you all accepted that you had a part to play and have the power to bring about the life you long for. There's success and there's failure; there's action and inaction. The universe is filled with opposites, precisely so we may have a choice."

Viola feels her irritation rise, like bile, from the pit of her stomach. The glimmer that begins in the back of her mind in response to his words is shut off by dark doors with years of honed practise. They snap shut before any hint of a new formulation can shimmer into being. "I have a big day ahead of me, so enough of this prattle. I need to rest."

The boy's manner changes. Viola admonishes herself. *That was harsher than it needed to be.* He bows with a flourish before slipping onto his sleeping mat and under the covers, turning his back to her. Viola prepares her bed and readies herself, thinking all the while.

Their first meeting drifts into her thoughts; he was a bag of bones then, a child hungering after more than food. He's changed much in the weeks they've travelled together. He's put on weight and muscle and is filling out. The skittish creature who in the beginning barely dared ask her a question has become an easy conversationalist, and now he's even arguing with her.

Viola shakes her head as she pulls the covers over her wiry frame. *He is trouble, that's what he is—trouble.* Why did she allow this to happen? Confusion tugs at her, and she rubs a hand over her brow. What is with her weakness when it comes to this boy? Why did she even allow him to accompany her that day? As she drifts between sleep and waking, thoughts filter into her semi-conscious mind. There's something about him. She knows it. Like that light shimmering around him when he tells stories. He is something unusual, life-changing.

Chapter Nine

The day dawns murky as always. Viola is not in a talkative mood. She keeps to herself, and the boy decides to mind his own business. He observes her, though, realising she's calmer and more collected. *Perhaps she did make progress yesterday. Maybe that's why she was finally willing to talk, even a little.*

He sighs. He's happy she's achieving what she wants, but a heaviness sweeps over him, weights to pull him down. He'll be on his own again soon and doesn't feel ready for it. *What have you got in store for me, Mother-Father? What am I going to do when she leaves?*

Sadness folds the petals of his heart into a closed bud. Hurt settles in his core. He finds solace in the garden at the centre of the inn. As always, he's the only patron there. *Why doesn't anyone else appreciate this place?* He glances up, watches the dark purple that swirls above. He feels a tickling sensation in the back of his throat. *Something must be done about this.* He spends his day thinking what he can do to combine his desire to clean the city and tell stories and survive on his own.

The light is low when Viola seeks him out. "Come," she instructs.

He follows her. She's wearing her large hat. The feather in it billows out above her head. He likes the way her short, russet cloak swirls about her when she walks. She has the air of a storyteller today, and he's grateful that he'll get to experience Viola's performance one more time. This is what drew him to her—what made him want to become her apprentice. The iron mantle he's borne all day crushes his spirits further. Isn't there some way he can keep following her? He knows it's her choice, and this time he must accept what she wants. Then he sighs and lets go. *I must leave this up to the wisdom of the higher order. If I'm meant to continue as her apprentice, it will be so, and if not, the Mother-Father will offer me something else—something even better.*

The load lifts from him, and he smiles for the first time that day. *Everything is going to work out perfectly; it always does. I can trust in that.*

He starts paying attention to his surroundings. As with the other districts he's passed in this city, the buildings are grey cubes, coated in the dust of the ash-cloud above. His eyes pick out a new detail. The streets they're walking through are clean. He glances about. They're near the tavern where he delivered his first story a few nights before. *This area was a disaster just a few days ago. Now it's swept and spruced up. Sure, there's a sheen of purple dust, but it isn't as thick as usual. How did that happen?* His heart fills with wonder at this change. A few blocks farther, the accumulated grime taints the streets again, becoming progressively worse.

Viola turns to him. "You have noticed it too. It was tidy back there by the tavern, even when the rest of the city is still dirty. The same thing happened around the marketplace the other day. Very interesting—"

He senses that she's insinuating something. "What do you mean, Master?"

She gives him a knowing smile but keeps walking in silence.

They turn a corner and the boy gasps. His feet slow in spite of himself. This street sparkles and the scale of it is beyond anything in his experience. Tall columns sweep high into the sky, holding imposing roofs on enormous buildings. Everything is scrubbed clean, and glowing crystals, sculpted into statues, light up the gleaming white façades of the magnificent edifices.

"Come along!" Viola pulls him out of his gaping wonder.

He follows her into one of the buildings where liveried attendants meet them at the carved wooden door. His gaze follows the entrance up and up. It's three times taller than he is. He feels the scrutiny of the attendants as their judgement reverberates through him. *Who am I to enter this place?*

"Welcome to the Merchants' Guild," Viola whispers as they're led through a sweeping hall and into a small side room. The floors are carpeted. His feet sink into the soft pile. He glances down and becomes aware of his worn sandals and scuffed trouser legs. The attendant instructs them to wait and wrinkles his nose as he passes the boy on his way out. The boy draws in on himself. He wishes he could vanish.

Viola lays a hand on his shoulder. "Never let them intimidate you," she instructs. "You are a storyteller of worth, and I know you bathed today. You are clean, and you take care of yourself. Your fortunes can change if you act the part and give them the best entertainment they have ever had. Once, I was in a similar situation. It is a question of believing in your ability and ignoring everything else. Their opinions are irrelevant if they're based on false assumptions."

He draws a deep breath and nods; he knows this. A smile creases his cheeks, and he feels himself grow taller again.

When he turns his attention to the room they're in, new words come flowing into his mind as they always do when he encounters unfamiliar things, but this time there are very many strange concepts. *Carpet. Electric light* —like gas lamps, but without the flame, just an eternal glow. *Portrait. Velvet curtain. Chaise longue. Wallpaper*— The list keeps growing.

A short while later, a different door opens, and they're led into a spacious hall that bustles with activity. Viola instructs him to remain in the shadows by the doorway while she climbs three wooden steps onto an illuminated platform. The gathering of people hushes in a slow ripple, starting at the front and working its way to the back. Viola stands tall. She's clothed in finest silk, a gown the shade of burgundy wine that migrates through all the solar hues until it ends in lemon yellow at her feet. He wonders when she changed because he's certain she didn't walk the streets in that dress.

Viola waits for silence. When the stillness in the room gathers to a tangible state, she leans forward and casts her voice into the furthest corners of the great hall. "Ladies and gentlemen, members of the illustrious Merchants' Guild, Citizens of Ilwych, on this occasion, you have the opportunity to hear a tale right from the heart of the empire."

She turns and perches atop an upholstered crystal stool, ball and claw feet carved with delicate care. The cascade of her skirts falls upon untainted white marble, smooth and pure, shimmering in the golden light cast from magical orbs that float above.

She launches into a tale the boy knows well. It's one of those she trained him in, but within moments, a series of lines creases above his nose. She's telling *The Destitute Countess* differently. She uses other words, places emphasis on different aspects, and develops certain elements in a new way. Realisation hits him. He glances out at the gathering in their beautiful silk gowns and slippered feet. *She's adapting the tale to the audience.*

As Viola's voice enchants the host of listeners, the boy's attention is caught up in the opulence surrounding him. His eyes reach the painting on the ceiling, a visual tale detailed in myriad colours. He stands beside a hundred other listeners, their silk outfits shimmering with threads of precious metals, their flowing head-coverings no more than a passing reminder of the climatic conditions beyond the hall. There's nothing practical about their clothes and head-scarves; everything is about being seen, being appreciated, and instilling awe.

New words bombard his brain. He crumples under the assault. His head pounds with all the information trying to squeeze its way in, all at the same time. To combat the attack on his senses, he forces his mind to focus on Viola, to listen to her tale, holding onto the only familiar thing in the room. The boy pays attention. He observes every change she makes and how it transforms the fable.

The original story is not about the trappings, the

external wealth, or the fine accoutrements. She adds these elements because they're what these people want to hear. The boy sucks air through his teeth. He realises there's more to the art than what you tell. How and to whom one does is also important. Another thought strikes him. She's telling a tale with a message running counter to the listeners' habits. The countess' tale is all about giving and being charitable, although Viola doesn't emphasise this aspect. Nevertheless, the boy doubts it's a thought that will ever cross these people's minds. The subtlety of his chosen craft settles into his consciousness.

Viola's voice drops for the ending, releasing her audience from the spell of her words. A collective intake of breath is followed by soft rustling. The hall erupts in clapping. A few subdued voices exclaim, "Bravo," or "Wonderful," and Viola bows.

When she straightens, she raises her hands, gesturing for quiet. The patrons settle, and she asks, "Could I interest you in some more entertainment?"

The crowd calls out their affirmation. She grins, and the boy senses her gaze on him. His stomach plummets into his feet at the mischievous glint in her eyes. *What is she going to do?* Panic slams its lightning-strike through him.

"In that case, I would like to introduce you to my apprentice. He is a very promising talent whom I met a few weeks ago in the dusty backwater of Fásach. He has a special offering for you today."

She beckons, but the boy is rooted to the spot. He can't bring himself to move. Viola's encouraging smile thaws him enough that he can lift his feet. In a trance, his body pouring cold sweat and his hands trembling, he steps onto the first stair, then the next one. His motions are disjointed. He reaches the top and makes his way to where Viola stands. He can hear the comments and sniggers out in the darkened hall, and he's grateful it's so bright on the stage that he can't make out the sea of faces below him.

Viola turns to him and murmurs, "Tell *The Shiptrader's Tale*. You know it well and have delivered it flawlessly to me. I shall be standing just down there." She points to the first row directly below him. "Just look at me, and you will be perfect."

He tries to respond, but a rock has lodged in the back of his throat. He squeezes his eyes shut to more laughter and takes a breath. His chest constricts, iron bands of fear holding him in their tight grasp. A second intake eases the pain. He opens his eyes and finds Viola in the gloom.

She nods, and he begins, stumbling over the first words. As he gets into the second sentence, his voice begins to grow, reaching beyond him and winging its way out into the hall, which falls silent. Eyes trained on Viola, he allows the practised words to flow. His brain is still a blank fog of panic, but his lips take over—they've done this before.

He senses his knees are weak and sits down on the ground. He speaks all the while, growing in confidence as he continues. Viola beams up at him, fanning his courage. All too soon, he comes to the end. He wakes as though from a dream. The reality of what he's just achieved hits him, and he reels. He's trembling—a leaf in an autumn breeze—and spots flash across his vision. He blinks. Then the silence is torn apart by tumultuous applause.

Viola is beside him, pulling him into a deep bow. They leave the stage together, and he's grateful for her hand supporting his elbow. They make it into the side-room before his legs give way. He sinks into the carpet, his fingers resting on the soft surface. Time is a disjointed series of impressions, which realign themselves when Viola stands before him wearing her usual clothes and the russet cloak.

"You did well," she says.

He focuses on the bright grin she offers him. *Is she smiling? I must be dreaming.*

"Up you get, boy. You did more than well. You have just secured yourself a place in this city. You captivated them."

He tries to stand, but his legs are still uncooperative.

"Why didn't you warn me?" His voice comes out as a high-pitched squeak.

"It would have been much worse if I had. When you don't have time to be afraid, you always succeed. Your practising paid off. That is all that matters."

She pulls him to his feet and hands him a pouch. Something clinks inside when it transfers, and the weight is unfamiliar to his fingers. "This is for your contribution this evening. You see, it pays well to be surprised."

Sticking his fingers into the opening at the top of the draw-string bag he pulls, gazing at the shiny coins within. They're silver and larger than any coins he's seen before. There are fifteen in all.

"Come along," Viola calls.

She stands by the doorway. Pulling the drawstrings closed again, he hurries to her side. The warm night air dispels what is left of his shock and the reality of what he's achieved sinks in. Soon, he's laughing with her about the whole experience. He gushes over the performance, and they spend an evening celebrating in the tavern where he first spoke.

A patron recognises him and requests a story, and the boy is on his feet in a flash. Standing before his second audience in the same night, he tells *The Sewing Princess*, finding the meaning in the tale he struggled with in weeks past.

More coins find their way to him, and he closes his

eyes for a moment of silent thanks. When Viola encourages him out of the tavern to cheers from the patrons, his thoughts turn to the gratitude he feels for this abundance with which he's been showered.

His steps falter halfway up the street as an idea comes to him. "Master," he says. She turns about, surprise flitting across her face to find him several paces behind her. He joins her, pulling the coin pouch from his pocket. He pulls out more than half and hands them to her. "Here, Master. Please accept this towards your needs. I have enough with what is here."

A frown scrunches up her face, and he notices a hint of guilt flitting through her eyes. "No. It is yours. Well-earned from hard work. I cannot accept it."

"I insist, Master. You have greater need of it than I do." She hesitates, so he adds, "Consider it a gift."

Viola swallows hard several times as she takes the eight coins he holds out to her. "Thank you," she manages in a hoarse voice.

He nods and smiles, continuing up the clean stretch of the road towards their inn. Then his eyes fall on a huddled figure lying on the ground. Tattered rags cover a thin body which is tinged with purple dust. The boy kneels beside the emaciated figure. He pulls out all the small coins from his evening's takings at the tavern and pushes them into the beggar's trembling claw.

"Here. Take this and go to the tavern over there," he

points back the way he came. "They have food, and they're still open."

"Dragons bless you!" the man croaks from behind chapped lips, hollow eyes glistening with emotion.

The boy nods, helps the beggar to his feet, and turns to continue his path towards the inn. Viola looks back and appraises him. He sees many questions crowding behind her eyes.

They start walking, and at length, she says, "You need to start taking better care of your finances, boy. If you don't watch out, you will be just as destitute as that man. You have to plan and budget and save so you don't find yourself unable to see to your needs."

"Master, what do you hear when you tell the tale of *The Destitute Countess*?"

She pauses, holding aside the screen at the inn's entrance to let him pass. "What do you mean? It is a story about a woman who achieves financial freedom after struggling with debt for years. It is clearly about success after tenaciously striving against all the odds."

He shakes his head, suppressing a laugh, as he skips up the stairs. Viola follows more slowly, every second step heavier than the one before it. When they reach the top, he meets her gaze. "The countess *gives* even when she has little. The Mother-Father rewards our generosity." He settles onto his sleeping pallet before continuing. "We're given a flow of abundance in many different forms. In this case, the flow is money, and it's our divine work to spread the wealth, only in that way can we open ourselves to greater plenty, because we, too, are acting in harmony with affluence." He kicks off his sandals, leaving them where they fall.

She bunks down after leaving her shoes and cloak neatly placed beside her sleeping place. She shakes her head, but he continues, ignoring her disagreement. "You, who plan and budget and *save*, do you ever achieve any income with a feeling of effortlessness?"

"No. It is hard work, obviously."

"It doesn't have to be that way. We can open ourselves to greater fluidity by being more open ourselves. I know —really know—that I will find ways to survive tomorrow and the day after; I just have to see the opportunities that come my way. When I focus on what I have and what I need, I don't see the lucky moments because I'm not in tune with what I want to accomplish. That man in the street was there because the Mother-Father wanted their child provided for and I was the tool used to make it happen. It's my duty to provide when I can so that, in turn, I can trust I will be provided for."

"I need to sleep."

He smiles at her habitual way of shutting down his words. Slipping out of his shirt, he thinks, *At least she's heard it*. He lies down and allows soporific waves to flow over him in slow eddies.

Chapter Ten

Viola wakes early. The darkness is so complete, her eyes are blind. She sits, fumbles for her clothes and dresses by touch alone, all the while listening to the rhythmic breathing of her travelling companion. Suppressing the voice within, which clamours to be heard —that cry driving guilt into her mind—Viola shuffles past the boy and out of the door into the half-lit corridor. She picks up a small satchel she left beside the door the night before, grateful the heavy backpack is already at her destination, and hurries out into the roadway, swinging a blue, floor-length cloak about her shoulders. She strides through sleeping streets, checking behind her at intervals.

Viola reaches the first turn and hurries around the corner when her conscience breaks through her defences, loud and demanding. She tries to suppress it once more but fails. Guilt racks her for having used him as a decoy and abandoning him now he's of no more use. In addition, he risks discovery when those hunting her realise her deception and search for two travellers. She knows they will eventually come after her, one way or another. *This is heartless.* Her steps slow; each stride is an effort of will.

It is what is best for him, she argues with herself. She's done all she can to provide him with a future in this place. Her conscience retaliates with force. *What good will that do when he gets tangled up in the game of cat and mouse?* He has nothing to do with this chase, but he's already in the thick of things. She dragged him into it, and there's no knowing what they'll do to him on account of her.

Viola stops in her tracks. She hesitates a moment before turning her feet back in the direction she's come. "Of all things unholy," she curses. "Confound him and his infernal moral compass!"

She flies through the streets, takes the stairs two at a time and barges into the room. "Up!" she exclaims, her chest heaving from the exertion of her run.

He grunts and rolls into a sitting position.

"Get up, boy!" she reiterates. "We must leave now. No questions. Just come." She spies his clothes, neatly folded beside him. "Quick!" She holds the shirt under his nose.

"Coming," he mumbles. He dresses while Viola paces, glancing out of the door every time she passes it.

He stands. "Ready," he whispers, and she tears back out into the street with him close on her heels.

Light filters through the dark cloud cover. Viola's heart leaps into her throat. *We are going to miss it for all this idiocy! And then where will we be?* She gasps for air and lengthens her stride. She has to hurry, has to make it. There's no other way. This is it; she must arrive in time.

Hurtling down the street, she's vaguely aware of the boy trailing her. Her mind jumps through the different options for getting to where they need to go, hoping to find a more direct route. *Go the way you know,* she insists. *That is the best. Cannot afford to get lost.*

They run. Viola hears their feet pounding on the rough stones of the streets. Her ears pick out the heaviness of her breathing and the faster pants coming from the boy. Her heart burns, stinging tears into her eyes, but she pushes on. She knows the pain is nothing if she can make it. Her entire being focuses on reaching a point on the far side of the city, by the docks.

Relief tugs at her when a large shadow looms behind a row of buildings. They're going to make it. Then her urgency reaches a new level. *Keep going. Do not take anything for granted. You only make it when you are there. Get there!*

Chapter Eleven

The boy fights to keep up with Viola. Her long legs propel her forward at a speed that reinforces the urgency of the moment. He knows he must stay with her. This is the answer to his prayers, and he's well aware that he's being tested, as though the Great Parent is measuring his resolve. *I want this more than anything*, he reiterates, speeding up his steps to stay abreast of Viola.

A large shadow comes into view. It fills the horizon, and the boy looks up at an enormous hulk of metal. He's never seen anything like it before, a great grey mountain of sheets and rivets, glimmering smooth, reflecting the thunderclouds above the city. He realises they're headed to the docks, that mythical place he heard some of the miners talking about the night before. Now the city buildings lie behind him; there's only a smooth, paved expanse between him and the incredible ship. He slows as awe fills him. The megalith towers into the sky, blotting out all else.

His attention is drawn back to Viola when he hears her shouting. The cry is followed by a deafening grating of steel on steel. The doors are closing, the gangway creeping away from the hull. Viola flings herself into the cavernous hole in the side of the ship and shouts for people to wait. The boy runs in earnest now. His feet fly across the paving, and then beat out a loud rat-a-tat-tat on the metal of the gangway which is still steadily moving away from the hull of the ship, all of its own accord. He sees the doors in the hull have ceased their closing, and he hears Viola's frantic pleading, "Please wait. Just a second. Wait!"

He gauges the distance and leaps, careening through the gap.

The boy lies on the cold, hard surface, gasping for air. Pins tear through his chest with each ragged intake. Tears seep out of the corners of his eyes, and relief floods him.

I made it! I just, just, did it. Viola's face swims into view above him.

"Come along. You can rest in the cabin." Her voice is brisk, as matter-of-fact as ever.

With a groan, he comes to his feet. He follows her

through winding, well-lit passages into the interior of the vessel. The whole megalith whines and creaks with the preparations for launching. If everything on the exterior of the vessel was grey, the interior is bright white. The sheer whiteness is blinding to his eyes accustomed to shades of brown. There's an emptiness to this place, devoid of living things. No animals. No plants. A man-made desert of light and smooth surfaces. He shivers at the sterile, stern, and desolate surroundings.

Viola pulls him through a doorway. The hatch slides shut behind him without a sound, and he looks about. It's a small room; everything is shiny white and illuminated. All the surfaces are smooth, reflecting the artificial light in a blinding array of glistening pearly surfaces. The room is devoid of comforts. A strange raised surface is located against the wall opposite the door. He can't recall ever having seen anything like it. The unbidden word that drifts into his mind is *bed*.

A sterile voice echoes out of nowhere, "All passengers, prepare for launch."

He can't make out whether it's a man or woman speaking. *Not that it matters*, he thinks, although an oddness in the timbre sends a shiver through his spine. "We launch in ten, nine, eight—" Mesmerised, he stands in the middle of the cabin and listens to the disembodied voice as it counts backwards.

"Hurry, boy!" Viola draws him out of his reverie. "Get

over here. And be quick about it." She pats the space beside her on the bed. "The empress only knows what would happen to you if you don't follow the safety instructions."

The boy does as he's told. As soon as his body comes to rest beside Viola, she fastens a constricting material over their chests and presses a glowing green button above their heads. A transparent bubble snaps shut, encasing them. More unfamiliar words drift into his conscious mind. *Sarcophagus. Coffin*. He shudders without understanding why.

"—two, one," the voice intones.

A deafening roar fills his ears. His head feels as though it might split. In the next instant, a tremendous force presses him downward, blowing the air from his body and crushing him to the base of the bed below him. For what seems an eternity, he can't even think. He lies there beside Viola, unable to move and barely able to breathe.

The whole world is coming to an end, he thinks, shutting his eyes while his hands ball into fists.

Viola chuckles beside him; the rainbow of sound makes him open his eyes. She's looking at him, a mischievous glint in her violet eyes. "You were terrified!" she exclaims, amusement lining her voice.

He sees the transparent bubble doesn't ensconce them anymore, and the tight belt about his chest has released. He sits up and blinks at Viola. *I don't understand anything.* "What is all this bedevilled magic?" he asks, still shaken by the whole experience.

Viola laughs even harder, tears leaking from her eyes. "Not magic. Ah, you country bumpkin! There is no magic in these things anymore, only what is called technology."

The boy remembers the elders from his village cursing the technology which makes their work all the more difficult because it speeds up the rate at which the empire destroys environments. He shrugs. There isn't much he can do about it. It will be better to focus on learning as much as he can, now that he's here.

Viola clears her throat, but when he looks up at her, her expression tells him she's at a loss for words. The emotions playing over her features, the muscles clenching and relaxing in her jaw, the frown pulling her eyebrows closer together, the lips that try to bring forth words which won't come.

He shakes his head, compassion brimming within him. "You don't need to explain, Master. You chose to take me with you on this adventure, and for that I'm grateful."

In answer, she throws up her hands and shakes her head, her short, straight hair fanning out. Then Viola's brow furrows even more deeply as she adds, "I owe you an explanation. I nearly chose to abandon you out there, and you deserve to know why. We are in this together now, and for that, I am sorry."

He holds her gaze but keeps silent.

Taking a deep breath, Viola continues, "I am a fugitive of the empire. I have fled the empress' hunters for decades, staying just a few steps ahead of them at all times. That is why I am always travelling. In many a year, I have not stayed in one place for longer than a few days. And still, they do not tire. I hear whispers of them dogging me at every step."

"The drone?" he asks.

"Yes."

"So why don't you use your magic to change your appearance and disappear?"

Her eyebrow arches into her forehead. "How do you know about that?"

He grins at her. "When we arrived in Ilwych, you put on some illusion to make the toll master think you were a man."

"Oh, yes, of course. I had forgotten about that." She pauses, looking at the boy as though gauging him. She throws up her hands and continues, "There are several reasons magic isn't a fail-safe option. Illusions like that sap energy. It is hard to sustain them for any length of time. Also, magic is the domain of a select few in the Haldrian Empire. It would raise serious questions if anyone knew I have arcane skills. I make a point of only using it when absolutely necessary."

He nods, pondering all she's said. The next question brims in his mind. "Why are they searching for you?"

She wets her lips, holding his gaze before her head shakes imperceptibly and she looks at her hands, wringing in her lap. "I am not ready for that. I shall tell you some other time. I owe you that much for dragging you into this mess."

The boy shakes his head, a grin splitting his face and crinkling the skin around his eyes. "I look forward to it." He pauses, thinking about what she's revealed. "Why did you need that speaking engagement last night?" Curiosity drives his question. He worries the pieces of a puzzle in his head, twisting them until they find their place, slotting them into each other to create the bigger picture he craves to understand.

"I needed to pay for passage on this ship. I knew I only had this small chance to get away this time. Of late, they have become better at keeping up. I knew I needed to get to a new planet. Not even joining up with you managed to throw them off my tracks for more than a few days. Well, it bought me the time I needed because it changed my usual pattern. It fooled them, just long enough."

He nods, satisfied, and turns his attention to the empty room again, but Viola's reaction snaps his mind back to her. "I just told you that I have used you, and nearly chose to leave you behind to a fate of interrogation by the empress' minions, and you don't even raise an eyebrow. What is wrong with you, boy?"

He smiles at her incredulous tone. "I'm here with you. What is there to be upset about? I'm quite simply grateful to the great Mother-Father for hearing my prayer and helping you see that I'm your apprentice, and nothing can change that."

Viola's mouth works, trying to find the words to respond to his nonchalant manner. She gives up, throwing her hands in the air, and muttering, "Incredible, just incredible."

"What good would it do if I went on about being abandoned and betrayed? You haven't done these things, although you may have thought them. I'm just glad you understood that I'm your apprentice, the right apprentice for you. You came back for me, and I'm here. Nothing else is important. Thank you, Master."

On the verge of retorting, Viola opens her mouth, but then the door slides open with a pop and a hiss. An imposing man, with a black beard so large that it's the determining feature of his face, strides into the room.

"What is the meaning of this?" he demands of Viola, his voice booming. "Not only are you late, and hold up my ship, but you even bring a stowaway—and in broad daylight too!"

Viola's manner changes in the blink of an eye. She bows low, softening every muscle in her body in deference to him. She smooths her voice to a cadence the boy finds unnatural, as she says, "Ah, Captain, I apologise. A rather sudden change of plans occurred this morning. I am certain we can work things out." She throws a winning smile at the man, adding, "My apprentice is quite a skilled—"

The captain scoffs, "Apprentice? So that's the term these days." His eyes harden, disgust consuming his features. "He's a bit young for you, ain't he?"

The captain's tone and words bring a rush of heat up the boy's neck, all the way to his ears. In but a moment he feels even his cheeks burning with shame and discomfort. It's Viola's forced smile, however, which brings angry bile rising from his stomach. She bows at the captain as though conspiring with him, sharing a secret only with him.

The boy sees the fury simmering in her eyes, but also the thought that she has no other choice. He wants to step forward between them. Then he hesitates a split second, terror gripping his limbs. *You must do this,* the soft voice within asserts. *The damage to Master Viola's standing must be minimised.*

Still, the boy pauses as he looks at the towering figure of the captain. *I can't take him on,* the boy thinks. *He's worse than—that man.* As the boy stands there, uncertain how to respond, the captain has continued to demean Viola and even threatens to have the boy thrown out for sneaking aboard. Again the boy's intuition encourages, *You must stand up to him, tell the truth as you see it.* He takes a step forward, placing himself between the angry captain and the cowering storyteller. The injunction, *obey your intuition,* strengthens his resolve.

"Captain," he says in a soft yet unwavering voice. "I'm aboard this ship of my own doing and entirely of my own accord. I followed my Master. Now I'm here, and you certainly have the power to do what you want with me. But I'm an able-bodied man—I'm fit, I'm young. I may not be the storyteller my Master is, but I'm a fair fabler. I can also be put to use in other ways aboard this ship for the duration of my Master's stay. When she disembarks, so shall I."

The captain stares at him. His eyes bulge while he appears uncertain how to respond to the boy's statement.

Before he can gather his thoughts, the boy smiles as he steps towards the door. "Please, sir, tell me where I should go, and I'll start my duties at once."

The burly man swallows hard, gathers his thoughts and responds, "Well, I suppose an extra pair of hands in the galley won't go amiss, and we could do with more entertainment of an evening." He shrugs away his confusion, instructs one of his attendants, standing at the doorway, to show the boy to an empty bunk and bring him to the cook after.

With a wink to Viola, the boy follows his assigned crew-woman to the galley as he marvels at the incredible smoothness of the white surfaces in the interior of this spacecraft which is taking him the Great-Parent-only-knows where.

Interlude

Monadir hurtles over the smooth, hard surface of the quay, coming to an abrupt halt. He springs from the hovercraft, letting go of the handlebars and allowing the vessel to sputter away from him. A ripple of slightly warmer air is all that remains of the spaceship and his prey. His rage echoes into the unforgiving purple clouds above him as a fleet of hovercrafts pours into the open space behind him. The mobilisation is pointless now. With clenched fists, he turns to the detachment waiting for his instructions. *What to do? At every turn, that infernal storyteller slips through my grasp.*

Turning to the squad of around forty law enforcement officials dressed in the flowing robes habitual on this ruined desertifying planet, Monadir orders, "Bring me the registration for that ship and all information regarding its planned trajectory, passengers, and cargo. I must know everything there is to know about it!"

A ripple runs through the group of men and women as Monadir turns back towards the desolate sandy expanse where, only a few minutes before, the enormous hulk of metal stood. *What can I do; how do I see through her tricks, and when will this interminable chase end?* His mind wanders over the past few months and his firm belief that he would finally catch up with his target. She has outwitted him at every turn—for years now.

If he doesn't get things right, and soon, he'll be replaced. They won't stand for another failure, and he knows he must apprehend her. Things can't continue as they are, and he won't let her ruin his career, forcing him to spend the end of his days in disgrace.

A loud beeping draws Monadir's attention to his wrist. He taps on the device, scanning the information projected into the air before his eyes. His fist clenches again in determination as he holds the thin silver band close to his mouth and instructs, "The storyteller has escaped again. She is aboard the Startraveller's Hope with its first port of call in Téarman. I shall make haste to follow in pursuit and shall attempt to reach the ship before it arrives at that destination. Do not allow anyone to disembark before she is apprehended."

Monadir rubs his wide, damp brow in frustration. His eyes close as he promises himself that he won't fail again.

He's made this promise to himself before—and what good did it bring? He's still out in these forsaken hinterlands, running on a fool's errand. Why do they want this storyteller captured? And why can't they provide the funds and forces necessary to do the job properly?

Anger writhes inside him. *Why does this keep happening to me? What did I ever do to deserve this failure? Why do the gods hate me so? I have tried and tried, but still, she gets away.*

With a big sigh, he opens his eyes again. He scans the now empty expanse of flagstones. The city's officers have returned to their duties; his chase was nothing more than an exciting interlude in their otherwise dreary existence.

His fingers run over a silver chain about his neck. A smile softens the stern features. He pats the amulet nestled under the layers of his clothing, the cool stone pressing against the bare skin of his chest. Then Monadir picks up his hover scooter and nods, *Yes. Soon; soon, I will return. I must. It has been long enough.*

PART II
VIOLA'S DREAM

Chapter Twelve

Viola sits in a quiet corner of the entertainment area. The round silver table gleams in the artificial light, and she breathes in the fragrant aroma of the hot beverage she cups in her hands. The scent drifts into her mind, taking her into a long-forgotten memory.

She sits in the cool shade of the garden. The breeze whispers through the branches overhead but doesn't reach her in the walled enclosure. A cup of kopi, her favourite drink, rests on the armrest of the bench. She listens to the chatter of finches in a bush behind her.

"Isperia!" whispers a voice from a secluded spot screened off by a hedge of abelias. The fragile blooms speckle the solid green wall with white dots. Her heart skips a beat, and she consciously

steadies her erratic breathing. Taking her cup, she walks over to the shrubbery, kopi mingling with the flowers' springtime aroma. Her black hair floats about her shoulders. Tendrils tickle her face, and she brushes them aside with a brisk motion.

"Yes?" Her question is laced with anticipation. She knows who waits for her here but pretends not to. It is a game that brings butterflies to her stomach and sends her heart galloping.

Dark eyes capture her gaze. They are bright with adoration. His features are angular, and she loves those sharp lines. His lips are soft and how she longs to kiss them—but never dares.

A sound startles Viola from her nostalgic musings. She looks up. The boy, her apprentice, settles onto the stool opposite. She notices that his eyes are like those she remembers from her daydream—intelligent and filled with devotion. A sigh brings the wave of despondency crashing back over her.

"Don't let it go," her apprentice whispers, leaning towards her. "Whatever it was you were thinking about made you so— What is the word—" He gestures with his left hand. "I'd say peaceful, but it's not quite right. You were happier than that."

She thinks for a moment. "Serene," she offers at length.

He nods, murmurs the word as if remembering a

long-forgotten friend, then looks at her with his unwavering stare. "Hold onto whatever it is that makes you serene. It was good to see you like that."

Viola shakes her head, her short hair bouncing about her ears. In the aftermath of her memory, she misses the weight it once had. "There is no point in dwelling on those things anymore. That time is gone, and there is no way I can get it back." She struggles to keep the bitterness out of her voice.

His lips quirk into a small smile. "You can't go back, that's true, but you can move forward. You can search for such feelings again. You know how serene feels, so you can experience it once more if you allow your choices to take you there."

"Oh great, now you are preaching about choices again. Yes, I made a choice once, and I have been regretting it ever since. Hunted my entire adult life because I decided to become a storyteller."

He holds her gaze but says nothing. She feels an overwhelming desire to speak to him, to open up and pour her whole heart out, but the whiplash of fear sinks its claws into her chest once more. Viola's teeth come down onto her lower lip, shutting off everything. It mirrors the closing of her heart.

He sighs and leans back, clutching at the base of his stool. His eyes trail the surface of the table. Allowing them to flicker up once, he says, "I suppose it's time I answered that question you asked our very first day walking together. I'm ready now."

She thinks back to that day in the blistering heat and dust, but before she can immerse herself in the memory, he begins his tale.

There's a community near Fásach that dedicate their efforts to righting the destruction brought by human nature. They consider themselves Children of the Great Parent and custodians of the wisdom brought to the people of a distant planet many millennia ago. They call themselves Arkyvn, The Children, and are a proud race. Their god-given mission is very challenging, especially as there are so few of them. The community in Fásach numbers fewer than fifty adults and children, but all have some talent that can be used to further their purpose.

Faced with repression from the empire, the community keeps a low profile and works on re-establishing the natural order that has been propelled out of balance by human activities. They take their task seriously. Over the decades, their village has migrated from place to place, always following the trail of what you call the blight. I didn't realise it as a child because I only saw the results of their cleaning, never the worst contamination. Every day, they're out in the blistering heat, caressing plants, running their toes through the sand and singing of light and beauty. They do all of it for the .

sake of purifying the Mother-Father's creation, but I didn't understand that.

One family of the Arkyvn is considered special. They're the chosen ones. Their bloodline is a divine gift to help The Children succeed in their task and to bring honour to the Mother-Father. This particular family is considered special because they have always produced the most talented members of the community. Their status has remained unbesmirched for generations. The first child of the current generation is a daughter. From an early age, she showed promise beyond even the wildest imaginings of the community's spiritual leader. She was a bright student and from the tender age of five devoted herself to the task of her people, helping eradicate the blight and bringing about changes you couldn't even imagine.

When her mother announced a second pregnancy, the entire community rejoiced. This child, result of that same blessed union, would be an even greater asset to them. The knowledge of the child's importance came to the spiritual leader of the group in a divine message from the Mother-

Father. The second child would bring them out of the darkness and achieve the Great Parent's vision for All That Is. The child was destined to be a wonder and bring the divine benediction to all who knew him.

Instead of bringing life, when that boy child was born, he brought death with him, and the father couldn't celebrate his son after suffering the loss of his beloved wife. Although he saw his son as a consolation, he began to question the great deity. In his heart, the father struggled to forgive the circumstances that had brought his son into the world. He laid his hopes on the prophecy and the promise of the boy's gift. When the boy grew and failed to present any abilities worthy of the community, his father hung his head in shame.

Anger, also, simmered within him as the years passed. The loss of a great woman, and her abilities to neutralise the steady progression of degradation and destruction, began to wear on everyone, while the boy who'd been promised as the saviour of All That Is failed to show any aptitude whatsoever.

The older the boy grew without showing any skill, the more the community turned away from him, excluding him from everything. They did not starve him, but they did not feed him either. Their sadness at the loss of his beloved mother, and his uselessness, combined into a wall, making him invisible to all except the other children. Torment followed. Day after day, they filled him with pain and shame, for he had no way of defending himself against their powerful skills. As he was the only one without any power, his sister delighted in inflicting what the children saw hidden in the adults' eyes. For the grown-ups wished to vent their frustration and disappointment, and in that desire, they became even more resentful, for it's an impure thought to wish harm on another child of the Great Parent.

Everyone knew what was happening, and they all turned a blind eye. No one cared; in their eyes, they were absolved because they inflicted no harm. The boy was not what the Mother-Father had promised them, and that meant he was a source of shame to be hidden away and ridiculed. Even the spiritual leader began to doubt his vision, claiming there was something defective with the boy who, for the prophecy to be false, must have angered the Great Parent in some way.

In the beginning, the boy escaped by taking care of livestock—ensuring he was far away from where the work of the others took them. He cared for the creatures and made them into his friends, but all the while, something within him longed for more. He loved words. They burned within him like the flicker of blue in a flame—always present right at the centre of his being. During festivals, when the holy man spoke, telling tales of the Great Parent and the messages the Prophetess brought to The Children, the boy who wasn't worthy of his name listened from the shadows beyond the fire, drinking in words, coveting each one. Alone in the valleys with sheep and goats for company, he shared his insights with the twin suns and came to know the greatness of the Mother-Father.

In whispers, he communed with his creator and realised he was not a failure and was meant to leave his people. This was why they had to shun him. It was why he'd been denied a mother's love. If he remained there, he couldn't fulfil his purpose. He was meant to leave, and everything was set into motion so he could choose to shoulder the burden and embrace the adventure before him.

He still does not understand the full extent of the plan—but who is he to question the Greater Wisdom? He trusts that a purpose does exist and all will be revealed in time. He has been blessed with a fortuitous meeting that sped him on his way, and he knows, deep down, all will come to pass as it must, for the Great

Parent wishes to see change, and that can only happen if a shift is brought about in all people. This boy must learn many things and see the empire before he can achieve his purpose.

As he speaks, his finger traces circles on the smooth surface of the table. He glances up at her, and Viola feels her heart constrict at the depth of pain in those dark wells. *He has been through that? So young and so vulnerable. How can anyone load so much on a child? And how has he come through it with such confidence?*

He shakes his head, holding her gaze. "I don't want pity. I know all that has gone before was to sculpt me and make me who I need to be. I can't do what I must—what the burning blue flame inside my heart wants of me—if I don't see the world, see the universe. The Mother-Father made things the way they were so I could leave—because I couldn't do what needs to be done by staying with my people. I could only do that with you, Master."

It is Viola's turn to shake her head. "It beggars belief how calm you are about it all. What about the injustice of it? What of cruelty? And your sister and her friends? How can adults stand by and watch an innocent child being tormented? Where is your anger, your resentment?"

"Those feelings can't help me." His words are soft and yet there's a power to them, shaking Viola to the core.

"But these are human reactions. They are normal."

He laughs. It is neither derisive nor judgemental. It is an expression of open freedom. "All reactions are linked to our thoughts. I don't think about such things because I know they can't lead me where I wish to go. I'm also not alone. I've had the guidance I needed to learn of other ways. The Great Parent has been by my side always, comforting me, guiding when necessary. When we spend much time with other humans who share these *natural reactions*, as you call them, they train each other to have these reflexes. I was blessed to observe humans from a distance and to learn to pay attention to other creatures too. Sheep don't hate wolves. They fear them, and they long to survive when the wolf comes after them, but they don't begrudge the wolf the need to eat either. That's why I don't resent."

He stands. "I must get ready. It's my turn to tell some tales and entertain the ship's guests. We can talk again tomorrow, if that will work for you, Master. I see you bear much, and I know I can help. Please let me support you in the only way I can. To share your burden is a blessing."

He turns and walks away, leaving Viola to ponder his words and marvel at his ability to brush off what life has handed him.

She remembers her cup, but it's cold now. She grimaces in distaste, pushing the offending brew away from her while her mind turns to the strange community he comes from. Was there such a thing as magic among men? She'd never heard of it, but he spoke of everyone in his community wielding special skills as though it were the most common thing. *He was the odd one out because he did not have magic.*

In a nearby alcove, the boy settles down in the company of a group of children and begins a tale.

Viola observes him from her vantage point. *I still cannot believe it is possible—it beggars belief that a man is able to wield supernatural powers.* Out of the corner of her eye, she notices a flicker of coloured light. She locks her gaze onto her apprentice. Another realisation stabs her. This one is earth-shattering, and she sits, numbed for a moment. *Regardless of the episode with the meerkats, he believes he has no magical powers. He also never notices what happens when he tells stories because, to protect him, I keep suppressing the visual manifestation of it. How can I let him know he does have magic?*

Under the table, out of sight from prying eyes, she weaves her hands through the air and the flickering shades that surround the boy disappear from view. She doesn't know if only those with magical powers can see this expression of his magic, but it's not worth the risk. If more found out, he could end up being carted back to The Capital as a curiosity or an experimental subject. She sighs. *I have to tell him somehow. And to think I bound his powers to him and they have already strengthened so much that they broke through the binding.*

She considers the situation and concludes that he's a manifestation of the impossible. *Maybe he is right to spout about being chosen by his god. No, no, I am letting my imagination get the better of me. Gods don't exist.* There cannot be a greater purpose; there is no greater power. She can only see avarice and extermination. Humans are a blight on the universe, and she knows they search for hope because they're desperate to justify their existence.

A bright seed of light pulses within her, objecting to the thoughts that invade her mind. A sigh parts her lips. *Well, maybe—just maybe—his understanding reflects some form of the truth even if I cannot see it myself.*

Viola turns her attention back to her life. She thinks about the years spent being hounded from place to place, constantly looking over her shoulder, always fearing capture. She remembers times she woke in the middle of the night, terror clawing at her throat, knowing they were upon her. Her mind plays over those innumerable times she crept out through a window, escaping just before swarms of hovercraft descended on the inn in which she was taking refuge.

The constant fear and worry changed her. She doesn't recognise herself anymore; she's become a grumpy old woman. The pleasure she used to get out of telling stories has dissipated, and she knows he's right. Enough is enough. *I don't know how I am going to do this, but I need to stop running. There has to be another way.*

Chapter Thirteen

The ship's bell blares the wake-up call into all areas of the worker's deck. Moans and griping emanate from most bunks, but the boy bounds out of his, ready to start another day. He's dressed and has his bed prepared before the others are even sitting up. While the crew stare out over the bunker room with bleary eyes, he prances through the illuminated sterile passages to the galley to begin his day's work. He can't help himself. Exuberance bubbles through him in effervescent surges.

One of his comrades calls after him that his bunk is a disgrace, but he waves off the criticism. He cares nothing for such expectations. The boy finds it funny how much time and energy everyone wastes on such unimportant things; he finds other concerns more valuable. Besides, the experience of living on a spaceship is fun.

The galley is a large space with many work surfaces.

Everything is sparkling clean and impossibly white. On his first day there, his mind, used to natural resources, is bombarded with a host of unfamiliar terms and objects that must be imprinted onto his memory. *Synthetic, rubber, sink, spigot, stove*— The overwhelming wave of information will continue for several days before his mind settles.

He now glances over the shelves on the walls; they contain dishes and crockpots. Pans hang from hooks above the main stove along the left wall. He makes his way to one of the work tables in the centre of the room where a pyramid of vegetables awaits him. He pulls a knife from the drawer under the surface and sets about his duties. The cook is a fat man with wobbly jowls and spotless blue overalls, and the boy listens as the man gives verbal instructions to the automated stove, setting the temperature just right for the telur he's making. More people filter into the galley.

The boy spends his mornings learning from anyone willing to share information with him. He never expected he'd like cooking. Before this, nourishment was exclusively a question of survival. Learning to create things with food, he embarks on an unexpected exploration of the glories of culinary skills. His eagerness exasperates some of the other galley staff, but on the whole, they enjoy his enthusiasm for their expertise.

Once he's completed his chores chopping vegetables and scrubbing pots, he enjoys a quick lunch break before heading up to the entertainment deck where he tells stories to the younger passengers before their dinner. The little group that assembles about him every day fills him with even greater excitement. He senses his meaning coming together as he recounts stories to these children who look up with wide eyes, wholeheartedly dragged into his tales, and always asking for more. He basks in this attention and the shift in his self-perception that comes with it. He isn't an outcast any longer.

One afternoon, on his way to the entertainment deck, the boy glances out of a porthole. The void of outer space draws his attention out into the silence—the intensity of its darkness spangled with glittering accumulations at distances so great that his brain shuts down when he tries to comprehend them. The serene beauty of the sight causes him to stand looking into the blackness, losing all sense of time.

Something shifts in his perceptions and he witnesses a thing of such magnitude that he'll remember it with every breath he takes and every beat of his heart, until his dying day. On the outskirts of a mass of stars, there's a shimmering light. It doesn't fit with what he knows about space. He watches in fascination as the light gathers to form an undulating, energetic creature with terrifying claws and bright, intelligent eyes. One huge luminescent eyeball stares right into him, and he gasps at the figure's terrible beauty. A shudder runs through him at the word that manifests in his mind—a terrifying, majestic and wondrous thing.

"There you are!"'

He starts and turns. Viola marches towards him. "You are late."

He glances back through the window but sees only stars glimmering in the darkness. "I thought I saw a dragon." His words are a whisper.

"A dragon?"

Her voice is disbelieving, confirming the impossibility of his claim, and his brows furrow as he vehemently, yet silently counters, *I know what I saw. I don't care if it's impossible. I saw a dragon.*

He walks off, Viola following behind until he reaches his habitual spot and settles cross-legged on the carpeted floor. A crescent of expectant faces gazes up at him. Gleeful questions and requests are thrown at him: "What is it today, Mr Storyteller?"; "Tell us the story about the knight again!"; "I want one about a princess!"; "Please, Mr Storyteller, another nice one."

His heart swells, and he smiles down at them, "Well, let me think. Hmmm." He hesitates, allowing their anticipation to grow until their bodies quiver with excitement. "What about *The Artist and his Muse?* Have you ever heard that one?" A chorus of "No!" is the reply and the boy beams at them.

He settles himself more comfortably, but as he opens

his mouth, an older woman cuts him off, censure and criticism dripping in her tone, "*The Artist and the Muse*? Is that even appropriate for children?"

The boy looks up from the youngsters to see a large woman of pale complexion dressed in a glittering gown so shiny it pains his eyes. He thinks fast, knowing the disapproval in her gaze could portend trouble. "Rest assured, Madame. It is a far cry from *The Showgirl*. You needn't fear for the virtue of these children." The woman's face turns scarlet as the other adults in the room titter their amusement at the retort. Hoping his quip will suffice, he turns his attention back to the little faces before him and begins his tale.

Later, when the children are ushered away to eat their dinner, he glances about. The woman who criticised him earlier is gone. He sees the captain striding towards him and begins to worry. His mind hops around from thought to thought, but before he can settle on a defence, the hulking man is upon him.

"I hear you're corrupting the innocence of children with fables unbefitting their age."

The boy swallows. What can he say? It is his word against that of an expensive sequinned gown.

The man bellows a laugh, making him jump. "Nothing to worry about, boy," the captain guffaws. "Madame Nichols is notorious around here for her pious vigilance on behalf of the other passengers. The children are happy, and that's all that matters. We wouldn't want the rascals bored and playing pranks on our very own *Ray of Devotion*." He rolls his eyes and grins at his reference to Mrs Nichols. "That would never do."

He pauses and the boy observes a gleam appear in his eyes. Then the Captain's face turns mock-serious, and he grumbles, "Now about that tale, *The Showgirl*; I'm sure the crew would love to hear that one after dinner." He winks and strides off, leaving the boy blinking in confusion.

A giggle startles him. He looks up, catching Viola's bemused look and does a double-take. Viola giggled?

"Your expression is too funny," she exclaims. "What did he want?"

The boy feels the heat of a blush creeping up his neck and lowers his gaze. "He wants me to tell *The Showgirl* to the crew after dinner." He runs a hand over the base of his skull.

"What?" Her eyes sparkle with laughter. "How did that come about?"

By the time he's told her of Mrs Nichols and her concerns, Viola's clutching her sides, laughing. She gulps in deep breaths, trying to still her mirth, but every time he glances at her, she bursts into peals of bubbling laughter. Still shaking, she takes him by the arm and leads him towards the mess hall.

Viola wipes the back of her other hand over her eyes

and sighs. "Well, I have not laughed like that in years. You are one to get yourself into amusing situations."

He shrugs. His ears are still burning, and as they collect their meal, he grasps at any opportunity to change the subject. "Yesterday, we started talking about what you'd like to transform in your life experience. Can we talk about it over dinner?"

She nods. "Yes, I think it is time I switch up my approach." She places her tray of food on a table, slips onto the bench, and leans forward conspiratorially, saying, "The time has come for me to tell you a story."

He settles down across from her, cutlery clinking as he smiles up into her violet gaze.

A young girl lived a sheltered life in the confines of her rich family home. She loved tales and spent hours reading massive collections. Whenever news of a visiting storyteller reached her ears, she would do everything possible to get her parents to invite the fabler to entertain them. As she grew older and expectations of her behaviour changed, she became argumentative. She only agreed to do what was wanted of her if she received opportunities to learn storytelling as well. Her parents allowed it—up to a point.

When she expressed her desire to become a storyteller and to practise the art, her parents flatly denied her. It wasn't a profession suited to her station, and they most certainly had no patience for it. All things related to storytelling were removed from her life, including the teacher they had employed. They insisted she had to prepare herself for the path they had already chosen for her and they refused to listen to her pleading. She was intended for a position of power in the empire, and there was no room for discussion.

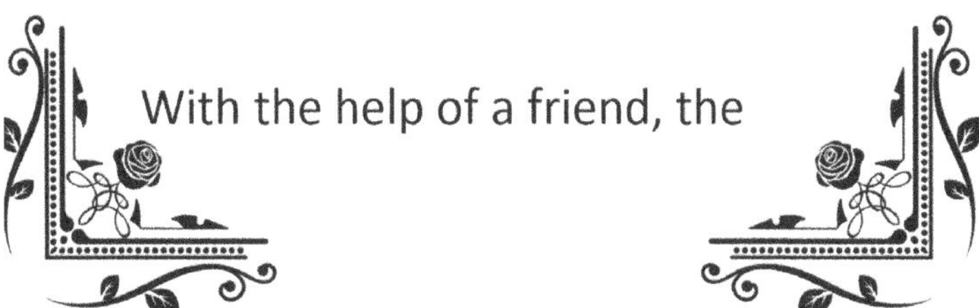

With the help of a friend, the

young woman fled her home and went after her dream. However, her family, being very powerful, searched for her, and in time imperial forces were pursuing her. Her mother was a force to be reckoned with, a powerful individual who did not take a snubbing, most especially not from her own daughter.

The boy's thoughts spread like a network of lightning through his mind. *Rich family— Position of power— Imperial forces—*

At Viola's sigh, he returns his focus to what she says next. "I thought if I could stay clear of them for a year or two, they would give up and leave me be, but they never did. It is close to thirty years that I have been on the run. Whenever I think I might have given them the slip, they find me again. It doesn't matter where in the empire I go, they always follow."

She closes her eyes. After gathering her thoughts, she continues, "I am so tired of it all. I wanted to tell stories, but I never really wanted to be a wandering storyteller, although that did have some charm in the beginning. Now I have almost come to hate recounting tales. Almost. It still brings me joy, but if I had known my family would cause such a hullabaloo, I would never have left. Now, I have been on the run so long that the tiredness and frustration are almost second nature. This is just how I live."

The weight of her experience settles into the pit of his stomach. He sucks air in through his teeth. *Powerful family with imperial connections,* he thinks. *No wonder she's so well educated and knows so much about the empire.* He tilts his head, thinking. "So, you still like telling stories, but you want to stop travelling. Is that right?"

"Yes." She pauses a moment, then elaborates. "I want to work somewhere where I can write the stories I have learned and share them more broadly. I like the act of recounting, but what's most important to me is sharing the stories. How I do it is less of an issue. Do you think I can stay in hiding and produce books in secret?"

"That might work. I'm sure there are other solutions you haven't even thought about, but let's start with what you want. You say sharing stories. Is there anything else?"

"Hmmm. I don't know."

"What about your knees and other joints? You

complain about pain sometimes."

"Well, I am getting on in years. It is to be expected. I spent most of my adult life on the run. I never took care of myself as I should. Yes, it has taken a toll, but I don't know what you expect from me; this is life."

He shakes his head. The desire to help bubbles within him, but he chooses to calm it. "You know that it doesn't have to be this way," is all he says.

"I suppose if I found a way to stay in one place, that would also make it easier."

"Any ideas about where?"

"Anywhere! As long as I could stay in one place for the rest of my life, I would be happy."

"So you don't mind being stuck in Fásach on Mshrali?"

"Heaven forbid, no! Too hot." He struggles to suppress a smile, and she laughs. "You are right. I suppose anywhere will not do. The best would be a temperate climate where my painful joints don't cause too much trouble. And of course, if I am staying in one place, it should be possible to get the affliction treated. Yes, that does sound nice."

He nods. "And what about others? Do you want someone else to be with you?"

Her face scrunches into a frown. "Since I left, I have done everything by myself. I could not bear having someone around all the time. You have tested me to my limits, you know. I don't think I could stand being around another person day in and day out. Especially not a man. Ugh. All the whining and complaining and "do this" and "get that done". No, I am a loner."

Another smile twitches his face into crinkles.

"Go ahead. Laugh!" she says sharply. "You will see. Being with another person is unbearable when you are not used to it."

"What about other forms of company, then? A pet, maybe?"

She stops her diatribe. "You know, I had a cat once. It was fun, but not quite my thing. Now a dog; a dog could be incredible—" She trails off, a dreamy look glazing her eyes.

"A dog it is, then," he says, bringing her back. "A place to live, a dog, and stories to set down in writing. Anything else?"

She shakes her head. Her eyes are gleaming. "A little cottage with a small garden to tend. A warm climate and taking care of myself. The opportunity to share my stories with a dog resting beside my desk. Taking walks and maybe getting to know my neighbours. That would be perfect."

"And so be it." He rises. "I have to get to the crew's mess hall now. I'm glad we could talk."

She nods, then she grins. "What are you going to do about *The Showgirl*?"

He feels his right eyebrow rise into his forehead. "What do you mean?"

"Well, it is quite tame. The captain is clearly looking for something a little saucier."

The toe of his boot becomes intriguing. "I don't—know," he stammers.

"Try to add bits here and there to meet the new expectation."

"How will I know how to do that?" He hears the shock and tension in his voice. "I'm thirteen! I don't know about any of that."

Viola shakes her head and pats him on the shoulder. "I have seen you in the mornings. You are a perfectly functional male. You will do fine. Just believe in the story. The rest will take care of itself as long as you let go enough to open up to possibilities." She waves her hand, encouraging him to get going.

He turns and walks away in a daze. Her matter-of-fact way of talking about this astounds him. *Why should it surprise me? Just because they never talked about such things in the community and frowned on the body's natural changes, doesn't mean it has to be that way everywhere.* He squares his shoulders and strides out the door with more courage than he feels. The pit of his stomach is still doing backflips, but with a deep breath, he pulls together his confidence. *Viola believes I can do it and the captain has requested it. I just have to get it right, somehow!*

Chapter Fourteen

Over the following days, Viola's spirits lift. When she sits up and stretches in her bed and the lights brighten, a rush of energy flows through her. She spends more and more time around the other guests and even partakes in the banter. She surprises herself by how often she laughs. It just bubbles out of her in an ever-increasing cascade.

When she's alone, Viola often thinks about the home she envisions for herself and the quiet life she longs for. The more her thoughts turn to the calm she dreams of, the more tranquil she feels. Her thoughts lull her into a sense of security. This journey with her apprentice is a wonderful change, and she relishes the serenity she experiences.

One morning, after breakfast, she requests a recording device from an attendant. Within moments of receiving the thin disk, she begins dictating. Stories flow out of her. Keeping a record of every story she can remember swells her energy levels further. She locks herself in her room for a few days and emerges invigorated, reverently carrying the device she borrowed.

She spies an attendant and crosses the entertainment deck to speak to the liveried woman. "Could I trouble you to transfer this onto a safe-keeper for me?"

The woman nods before taking the device and disappearing down a hallway.

While Viola waits, her thoughts begin a dance in her mind. At first tentative, but ever more daring with every pass, doubt plagues her. *What's the purpose anyway? How is this going to serve anything? How can the dream of a home and peace and quiet ever work out?*

As minutes pass, she brushes aside her attempts to answer those questions, and turmoil stirs within her. Impossibilities materialise, criticism surfaces; the longer she waits, the more certain she becomes that her wishes are nothing more than dreams—intangible, impossible to realise, and quite simply out of reach. *I am never going to achieve that. It is a silly fancy, nothing more. My reality is to be hounded my entire life or to go back in chains and do whatever they decide for me.*

By the time the attendant returns with a walnut-sized trinket, Viola's shoulders are hunched, and she hangs her head. She hardly notices she's chewing on a nail. She wants to fling the proffered item from her—a reminder of her disappointment. Instead, she slips it into her pocket to keep, just in case.

Viola turns around, searching the area. Groups of people are laughing and talking, children play, and she's reminded of how she doesn't fit in here at all. These folk have calm lives filled with mundane worries. They're rich traders and businessmen who accrue their wealth at the expense of others and the planets colonised by the empire. The underlying cause of the blight is their disinterest in the way their wealth is generated—not that she can blame them. They're the product of their society, and what incentive is there for them to care about anything beyond their own welfare? No one in The Capital seems to care how wealth is generated, as long as peace and prosperity are maintained, and the imperial family receives its cut. She, on the other hand, is a fugitive. When she forms attachments to other people, she puts them in danger.

The world spins about her, going faster and faster. She holds onto the back of a chair to stop the vortex from dragging her to her knees. Her heart pounds so loudly that it's the only thing she hears. She struggles to breathe. Her mouth is dry.

Then a hand steadies her. "It's going to be all right, Master."

Her mind clings to the familiar voice to stop herself

from drowning in the maelstrom of her anxiety. Air finds its way into her burning lungs, and she closes her eyes. The small hand under her elbow grounds her, reminding her she's not alone. This boy—she often forgets just how young he is—who's been through so much, is with her. Another inhale reaches her, clearing her mind. The vice-like grip of fear loosens and dissipates.

She can see and hear again. Children shriek and laugh in the middle of a game. The boy settles her into the chair. "Sit, Master," he encourages. His voice is different from usual.

He is so serious, she realises.

"Every day, the Mother-Father offers you a question. What will you do with this time, this life you've been given? And only you can answer it for yourself. To make the choice, you must learn to follow the light in your heart."

She blinks. Her mind is still muddied, and she snaps. "Stop speaking in riddles, boy."

His habitual grin creases his face. "You're back to normal. That's good. It looked like you'd given in to all the dark thoughts—those questions that try to tear apart the things you like, the things you want. You will be able to fight the shadows when you listen to what your heart has to say."

She shakes her head. "I don't know what you mean. It is all pointless. I am never going to get a place of my own.

This is the Haldrian Empire we are talking about. I am a fugitive, and they will never let me get away. Perhaps I should just turn myself in."

He brings his face very close to hers. His words are soft. "You can go ahead and believe that if you want to, but only if you want to. I know you can achieve it, even if, right now, it seems the obstacles are very great."

She frowns at him. *Why does he always have to be so irritating and contrary? How does he have an answer for everything?*

"We're all children of the Great Parent. The Mother-Father wants us to succeed but also gives us the freedom to choose our own way, to make our path, and in doing so, to shine more brightly because when we get it right, we know in our hearts that it *is* meant to be. Remember when you told me I couldn't become your apprentice?"

A part of her rails against this. She wants to push him away and leave, but something stops her—a thought steps in. *Listen. This could be important.* So she nods her head, and the boy continues.

"I listened to the small voice in my heart that said it was meant to be. I didn't know how it could. You kept insisting it was never going to happen, but I persevered because I trusted the light inside me. I knew I could follow what the small voice said because it comes from here," he taps his right hand to his chest, "and it would help me find a way to get what I wanted." He throws up his hands in a grand gesture. "And here I am, on a spaceship, with you, Master."

His enthusiasm is infectious, and Viola smiles, despite herself. "Fair enough," she acknowledges. "But how can this voice help me? It doesn't change the fact that I am a fugitive of the Haldrian Empire, which is so great and powerful that I cannot leave it. Trust me; I have tried. Even the planets on the very outskirts, where most people are left in peace and barely know anything of the empress, even they could not shelter me."

He nods, sitting down across from her. "When your heart knows what you would really like, and you let the light that's within you shine and fill the wish with brightness, then the Great Parent can do their part. *Ask, and you shall receive.* You need to be specific in what you're asking for, and you need to give it time to work. Once you know what you want, opportunities don't appear right away. You also need to be patient.

"It can be simple—even if it seems difficult from where you stand right now. But it doesn't have to be impossible. Allow the Mother-Father to work through you; embrace your nature as a divine child and let the power within you do its work towards your heart's desire. Because your true purpose can never go against the Greater Laws. We're all tuned into the Harmony That Is and we're happiest when we align with it."

She stares at him. *Who would have known this little boy*

could be so profound? She reflects that his religious babblings don't bother her so much anymore. *That is strange. What changed?*

While she ponders the answer, he takes her silence as an opportunity to continue. "Master, your doubts and fears are telling you that you've never achieved this before, but does that mean you can never do it?"

She thinks about that for a moment before answering, and she senses her eyes wavering under his intense gaze. "I don't know. But I suppose, if I think about the times I did new things, they often appeared impossible just because I had never done them before. Speaking in front of my first crowd was like that. I needed to do it for the money, but I was terrified and almost bumbled the whole thing."

"But you didn't bumble the second time, did you?"

"True. I was still afraid, though."

"When you brought me to this ship, and I watched the doors closing and the gangplank moving away from the vessel, I was terrified. I was scared of boarding this enormous spaceship, I was afraid of losing you as my teacher, and I was worried about whatever it was that drove your fear. I was even terrified of that jump I needed to make, but I didn't have time to listen to my thoughts. All I could do was take the leap and hope for the best. And I did do it."

She nods. Light-hearted bubbles begin drifting within

her, bringing a better state of mind with them. "I suppose you are right. I must *want* to take a leap away from my standard experience. Maybe I can stop thinking about being followed all the time. Do you really believe it is possible?"

"Absolutely!" His eyes shine with a bright inner light, and she smiles in return.

She's about to thank him when another thought draws her brows together. "Your not having a name isn't going to work anymore. I cannot keep calling you *boy*. What is it to be?"

He thinks for a moment. "Jo," he says at length. "Jo will be fine."

Chapter Fifteen

Jo spends a lot of time thinking about Viola. He wonders how he can help her see that she is worthy of the change she longs for in her life. He observes the moments when motivation surges through her, and she becomes a whirlwind of activity, but then a wayward gust of something else knocks her off-kilter. Every so often, he has to rush over and pick up the shattered pieces of her enthusiasm, trying to drag them from the clutches of depression that turn her world grey.

He stares out of the porthole at every opportunity he gets. Today he's thinking, not searching for glimpses of dragons—which he hasn't seen again. His memory plays with the moment when Viola surprised him at the Merchants' Guild. *I only managed to tell a good story because she believed in me. If she hadn't been there, I would undoubtedly have failed. How can I help her succeed?*

The blackness of deep space draws his gaze out into the void. The enormity of the universe stretches before him, pinpricks speckling the creator's jet canvas with light. Colourful nebulae swirl their cloudy mist over the darkness. Faced with this, he feels small and insignificant. It is vast, terrifying, life-threatening, but also immeasurably beautiful. *This is something worth protecting too. It may be so much bigger than I am, but I'm still a part of the universe, and because it's my home, I must do my bit— What is my part to play in all of this?*

The existential question takes him by surprise. Jo blinks at how it weighs on him. The question is important at a profound level. A disconnected thought flares through his mind, one of the injunctions of his people: *Speak the truth as you know it.* It floats for a moment, suspended in time, then an overwhelming series of images pours forth. Golden threads of an interconnected web tie him to all living things. He sees Viola, a ship drifting on the tide, cut free from her golden anchor. *She has lost her way.*

Clarity smooths the ripples of his mind, transforming it into a pristine, reflective lake. *I need to speak with the Master. This could be what she needs to break through her negative cycles. She was on the deck last time I saw her.*

He scours the sterile ship, running through white tube-shaped corridors, searching the smooth open areas separated by low couches or a sprinkling of tables here and there. At long last, he finds her in her cabin. She sits on the edge of her white bed, her arms cradling her head. Light shimmers off the walls, enhancing the stark utility of the space. There's no furniture, no sense of belonging. It's just a place to sleep.

Viola sits hunched over her knees and mutters to herself, her voice hard and intense. Jo's heart beats faster, and he wants to reach out to her.

He drops his arm to his side, recoiling from the hostility he fears he will receive if he touches her. Instead, he whispers, "Master."

She looks up. The coldness in her violet eyes pierces through his core. He shivers. *How do I do this?* he wonders.

"Master—" Words dry up in the back of his throat. His crystalline image of continuity shrivels under the pestilent clouds of her intense stare. He tries to catch himself, but only half-thoughts express themselves. "I— um— There's a— I—"

The area between her brows turns into a field of vertical lines. "Either you say what you have come to say, or you shut it. Stop blathering and get to it or get out!" she snaps.

His courage scurries out of reach into the pit of his stomach somewhere. He feels his trained reaction rearing its head, spinning him around and wanting to bustle him out the door, but he hits his chest hard and stops himself.

That may be how things were when I was a child, but I'm not there anymore. I don't have to behave that way here. I also know she doesn't mean it—not really. He can see she's slipping back into a shell of her own making, the habits that protected her all this time are her familiar territory, just like he used to slink about in the shadows. Jo realises he has to show he's embraced what the Great Parent wants for him and prove he's learned the lesson. *I have to be her beacon.*

Two deep breaths steady him, and he meets her gaze head-on. "There's an ordinance of the Mother-Father that says, 'Listen to the truth of others'. I would like you please to listen while I follow another ordinance, 'Speak the truth as you know it'."

She rolls her eyes but says nothing, so he inhales another calming breath, takes a few steps further into the room, and soldiers on. "When I decided to leave the place that was never my home, I didn't know how things were going to work out. I didn't even know where my next meal was going to come from. A part of me kept saying I'd never make it. I was going to die alone and shunned, belonging nowhere and to no one: useless, hopeless and meaningless. I felt as if everything the community thought of me was true, but there was another voice, the one that often speaks to me quietly and that encouraged my decision to leave. It said I could trust the Great Parent to take care of me, to see to it that I'd always receive the opportunities I needed. All I have to do is be prepared to take those chances. I have to be able to see the fair winds that will drive me towards what I want and know how to make the most of them. That's all.

"It turns out that my little voice was far more truthful than all the loud, panicked thoughts that boiled inside me. You can trust the voice of your intuition. The Great Parent provides. You can trust in that. I'm grateful every day for meeting you. I haven't wanted for anything since that moment, and I thank the Mother-Father for it. Please, Master, turn away from the lies and distortions you conjure in your mind. Remember that even the rain is a good thing. How would the plants grow without it? So when the clouds begin to gather, bless them and from the situation seek the rain—whatever it is—that provides an opportunity for growth. You can overcome your worries and doubts; I know it. Just like you knew I could perform a tale to the Merchants Guild of Ilwych before I knew I could, I'm certain you can have that house and that life of peace, but you, too, must learn to believe it possible."

She glares at him, her face flat and hard. He senses a wall being laid between them, brick by brick. She shakes her head. "How can I believe any of that when I have spent all these years running and hiding and being hounded down, time after time? I brought this on myself because I betrayed my family's expectations when I left. They are clearly not willing to give up on that, so I shall never be able to stop running. Peace and quiet are an impossibility. There are only two outcomes: getting caught or staying one step ahead of the baying dogs. My *dream*, as you call it, is insanity. It is impossible."

His heart constricts. *How do I make Viola see?* Then a thought strikes, and he goes with it. "Before you decided to leave, how impossible was your dream of becoming a storyteller?"

She sits up, a quizzical frown wrinkling her forehead. "I don't know—" She pauses, listening to some inner confrontation. "Yes, I suppose you are right. In the beginning, when everyone said I would not be allowed to and my parents dismissed my teacher, I believed it was impossible. Then my stubborn streak ignited, and I simply left."

He nods, excitement at the breakthrough emboldening him. "Once you made the decision, things started conspiring to make it happen, didn't they?"

"Yes, I suppose opportunities that did not exist before kind of showed up, just like that."

"If it worked for you then, and it's worked for me many times, can you trust in that? Will you keep running, or are you ready to try something different?"

Her head twitches in the slightest of nods. Tension lifts from him and his lips turn heavenward. "Master, can you find five things that were good about the years you spent running?"

Her eyebrows fly upward. Disbelief has her mouth agape. "Good things? Are you even listening to yourself? This is unbelievable," she exclaims.

"Yes, anything that was positive. A fire may burn and destroy the landscape but also brings with it the opportunity for renewal. What good came from your years travelling?"

"Um— I don't know." She brushes a hand over her face. "I have never thought of it that way before. I suppose—yes, experiencing the empire in all its sordid glory has been informative and fun."

Her eyes begin to twinkle, and he sends her an encouraging smile. She continues. "I like telling tales to different groups. It is wondrous to finetune them to the audience. Oh yes, and the time I stopped a tavern brawl and the innkeeper gifted me with my magically-charged quartz. Then there was the time I met a wandering fighter who insisted on keeping me company and training me until I could defend myself—because he did not like the idea of a young woman travelling on her own unable to do so. He was such a sweet dear."

She drifts away for a moment, wandering paths in her mind. Then she turns back and faces him. Jo observes her whole being lift and lighten, and as strong and unbreakable as it has been, the wall between them dissipates. She is different now. There's something bright and alive about her.

Eyes sparkling, she smiles. "Thank you, Jo. You have proven you are right, and still I keep slipping back into that place of panic."

Next step, he thinks and presses on. "Do you believe that you deserve to be hunted because you betrayed your family's expectations?"

She blinks. "Um— I suppose not— No. You are right. No, I do not; it is not true. Why did I saddle myself with such an odd notion?"

His shoulders rise in a shrug. "We can think the strangest things when we stop listening to the truth that's in our hearts. You also said there were only two options. Can you maybe think of some others?"

Silence stretches between them, and it's comfortable; there's a sense of growing companionship in the air. At length, Viola says, "I could go back of my own free will. I know I instinctively feel that I have no right to do so since I left and was disowned—but when I look past that, it seems like an amusing thing to do because they will least expect it. There is, of course, also the option of changing my name again and disappearing precisely by settling down and doing what they don't expect. Although, there is a risk they might find me—"

Jo nods. He is satisfied. She is glowing now, and peace

has settled over her, a snug cloak keeping out the cold of her dark thoughts.

"And what of that house and the opportunity to write and share your stories in a different way?"

"It seems like a better idea than ever." Her head tilts sideways with a new thought striking through her. "What about you? When I settle down in my little cottage with a dog, what will you do?"

He shrugs. "I'll know by the time we get there. I trust the Mother-Father—"

He is cut off by the tinny voice of the ship speaking into the room.

Chapter Sixteen

"Viola Alerion," the hollow voice permeates the cabin. "You are commanded to the bridge. Immediately."

Viola sits up. Alarm bells begin ringing in her head and her stomach clenches. Her heart and mind start racing. *The bridge. That means a direct order from the captain.* Dread, her constant companion for many years, invades her senses. It oozes a thick pool into her stomach. *Trouble,* the voice of her intuition says, without a hint of doubt. *Grab bags; be ready for anything.*

She flies to her feet, presses hard on a wall partition and begins flinging her belongings into the backpack which was stowed on the lowest shelf. In less than a minute, she's packed and striding out through the door, slinging the pack onto her back.

"Clear this room," she calls over her shoulder, hoping the ship's artificial intelligence can grasp the instruction.

Viola hears pattering footsteps keeping pace with her. Although her heart pounds in her ears, she is grateful for her apprentice. *What trouble am I dragging him into now?* The weight of worry becomes a heavy stone plummeting inside her. If they've managed to catch up with the vessel, she knows he's in as much trouble as she is. How did they find her? She covered all their tracks, and they were in Ilwych less than a week. *Why does this always have to happen? Why, just when I believe I might be able to find some peace, do they manage to catch up with me? And how am I going to get out of this one? We are on a spaceship! There is nowhere to flee to.*

Panic turns her thoughts into crickets. They hop from one thing to the next while she struggles to get her bearings, realising she has only a vague idea of the bridge's location.

Viola slows at an intersection. Casting about her, she hopes to spot a crew member, but the corridors are all void. Bright light and the humming of the ship's engines fill the silence. Hysteria begins to tug at the extremities of her mind, sending her heart racing even faster and forcing her breaths into gasping pants.

A small hand settles into the crook of her arm. "Breathe," Jo says. His voice is soft, and there's so much compassion in it. In answer to his encouragement, air pours into her lungs. The fuzziness brought on by the overpowering surge of panic settles—the ripples in the pool still, transforming into a perfect reflective surface.

Her memory calls up a lesson from many years before. An exercise given to a younger version of herself who now barely exists. *"Isperia, here is the blueprint of the empress' new flagship. We have discussed the basics of the physics behind space travel. Today let us take a look at what that means for the design of ships."* Within seconds, her mind recalls the three-dimensional hologram she spent hours poring over in detail.

Viola's heart begins to flutter with excitement similar to her experience then, but now it's because she realises how near to her destination she is. She pats Jo's hand to let him know she's all right, and then she sets off up a corridor. A few turns later, the sounds of activity filter through to her. Following the noise, she picks up pace again.

She pushes into a wide open space where flashing lights, enormous control panels, and a number of monitors bombard her with information. Crew members are talking, dashing about, and Viola picks up on their tension. Some of them stare at a monitor, their eyes wide, and her attention drifts to the image projected there. Several fast-moving red specks streak across the surface. They close in on a blue dot, which she imagines is the ship she's on. It lumbers in comparison to the red lights and Viola realises they'll be upon her within the hour. On a second monitor, she picks out the curve of a planet. *We are so close!* The realisation dashes her hopes into froth on the sheer rocks of life's adversity. *Why? When we are so close!*

A movement from her right draws her attention to the captain, who strides over to her. He crowds his huge frame into her personal space, bringing his livid face right up to hers, their noses almost touching. "How dare you put my ship in danger!" Flecks of spit fly from his lips and Viola exerts all her control not to step back and wipe her face. "I should have listened to my gut feeling to deny your petition when you asked for passage. Something about you was off. I knew you were trouble. Now look where you've got us. Hunted by imperial fighters like a pack of rebels." He gesticulates towards the red dots on the monitor.

Next, he shoves a meaty finger into her chest and demands, "You are going to tell me exactly what's going on, and you are going to fix this."

Over the communications system, Viola hears a voice distorted by static. "We requested to speak with the captain of the Startraveller's Hope, and our patience is running out. In the name of the empress and the glorious Haldrian Empire, we demand to speak with the captain regarding one of his passengers."

Viola hears the captain grind his teeth. He bellows at

his crew, "Put them off for a few more minutes. Placate them. Do anything you can to stall them." Then he turns his attention back to Viola. "Now, storyteller, why are you running from the empire?"

A jumble of thoughts piles through Viola's mind. *Have they actually stated they are looking for me? Could there be another passenger on this ship they might be out after? I cannot tell the full truth; he would hand me back in the twinkling of an eye if he knew my former identity.* She breathes and takes one step backwards, then she meets his gaze and goes as close to the truth as she dares.

Her voice is calm acid when she speaks. "I run because I am chased. I do not fully understand why they are after me. I have never allowed them close enough to let me know. I suspect it has something to do with my family and my decision, in my youth, to renounce all ties and take up the life of an adventuring fabler. I shall admit it never sat well with my mother, and this particular chase has been ongoing ever since. I had no intention of getting your ship involved in this, and for that, I am truly sorry."

The captain's dark eyes fly wide open as she speaks. His fish-faced expression calls forth a stifled snort from behind Viola, but she exerts all her willpower not to turn on her apprentice.

When he's composed himself, the captain bows. His voice is strained when he speaks. "My Lady, how do you wish to proceed? The Startraveller's Hope is at your command." He lays a hand over his heart.

Viola senses her right eyebrow arch. *This is unexpected.*

He responds to her unasked question in a whisper. "In the year 153 of our empire, all ships received a missive about a royal fugitive. By the shade of your eyes, I know you, Lady. Although I do not wish to risk the empress' wrath, you outrank them." He jerks with his head towards the red dots on the screen. "Protocol demands that I follow rank." His voice is grim.

Viola recognises a hint of resentment. Handing over his command to her doesn't sit well at all, and yet, she realises, because of the imperial system, he is bound to defer to her. She swallows. "What happens to you and everyone on this ship if you choose to harbour me and help me escape onto Téarman?"

The captain sucks air through his teeth. She can see how hard this is for him. "We become traitors to the empire and face the standard punishment for treason."

"Just you? Or everyone?" This is curiosity. She's never considered who might be affected by her rebellious act against her family.

"I can't be certain, Lady. But other extreme cases have extrapolated blame by association."

Her stomach clenches. A cold sweat breaks out, and she wipes her palms on her trousers. "I suppose you will have to turn me in then, but I want you to take this boy under your wing and care for him until he chooses to leave. He is an orphan and has no one to turn to. If I am to go back to The Capital, I want him, at least, to be safe."

Viola's heart wrenches at her own words. She doesn't want to go back. She doesn't want to see her mother's face again. The words *If you go, you will never be welcome here ever again!* ring in her ears. With firm resolve, she forces away the clamouring panic. *I am backed into a corner. I cannot risk everyone on this ship suffering for my sake—especially not for a childish whim I have outgrown. If it is time, it is time.*

The captain nods. "Your wish is my command, Lady."

A small smile twitches into existence as her spirits lighten, unable to suppress the thought that he still doesn't know who she is. Considering everything, she understands they probably just gave out a description and some instructions to return "the girl" to her family, without admitting to her name. *Ah, mother. The things you do to protect yourself and your position. And how others suffer because of it.*

Sadness pulls its blanket over her, only to be cast aside by terror once more when a small firm voice states, "I choose to go with my Master, no matter where circumstances take her."

Viola blots out the light, clenching her fist to keep at bay her fear for him. Then she turns anxiety to anger, as she's practised doing for many years. She faces him. "You don't know what you speak of, boy! I refuse to let you throw away your freedom in this way. It is not a topic for discussion."

He grins at her. It's his familiar cocky response to her fury. "I don't know what's going to happen in the next few hours, but your decision is a noble one, Master, and I understand your wish to protect. My heart tells me you're obeying your intuition and doing what you know to be right, no matter how terrifying that is to you. I also know you need a friend through this trying time, and I have nowhere else I need to be. It won't surprise you that I believe the Great Parent will help us out of this one if we're prepared to see the opportunities that come our way."

So naive, she thinks, shaking her head. "No. You are staying on board this ship, and that is final. I cannot saddle my conscience with this."

There's a flicker in his eye. She senses he wants to retort with something, but then he glances at the captain and bites back what he's about to say. Viola recognises the signs of frustration pricking tears in the corners of his eyes and his hands balling into fists. He turns away from her and Viola takes in the captain once more. He has marched over and is speaking through the communications device. His voice is low, and Viola can't make out his words, nor the crackled responses he gets, which are not being blasted throughout the bridge anymore.

Self-preservation begins gnawing at the edges of her mind. It wants to weaken her resolve, but her heart stands firm on this one. She won't allow others to suffer because of her. When it was just her facing hardships—that was one thing—but she knows change has to come and she decides to take her stand here and now.

A short while later, the captain approaches. Viola notices the change in his stance. His motions are softer, and he stoops, his eyes radiating deference. She appraises him and wonders what he's thinking about this wandering storyteller with the privileged family name. *If things were not so serious, it would be funny. Why does who my parents are make such a difference? I am forty-eight, for Emperor's sake! Can I not just be treated with respect? Aren't we all humans?*

Viola senses her irritation rising. She pushes against it, trying to keep it under, but struggling with this ball-in-water emotion. The captain's words draw her thoughts away from her inner questions and their resulting turmoil. She pulls her mind free from her considerations and focuses on what he says.

"My Lady, they agree to treat us fairly on condition you don't try to escape. They've instructed me to land the ship in Baile, where a delegation will meet you. Considering the situation and that you're now a distinguished guest upon this ship, I'd like to offer you my cabin for the remainder of your journey."

He licks his lips, pausing for a moment. Viola holds her council. She's fighting her demons, questions and doubts flaring like a thousand fires she has to put out one at a time. She manages to nod. His eyes flicker to her apprentice, and he adds, "As we agreed earlier, the boy is under my protection until such a time as he chooses to leave this ship of his own accord."

A weight lifts from Viola's shoulders. At least he will have the opportunity to find his way. Of course, there's the matter of his training, but she has an idea. She knows someone who could take over and considers that it may be best, after all, to send him on to someone with a quieter life.

She nods and clears her voice. It still rasps when she says, "Lead the way. I humbly accept your offer of the cabin until we land."

He nods and motions for one of his crew to lead Viola. She leaves without looking back. When she hears the doors to the bridge slide shut behind her, it feels as though a chapter of her life has also come to a close. *What happens now? What will all these long years of fruitless running bring me? What was the point of any of it?*

Chapter Seventeen

Jo stands aside, listening to the agreement that Viola and the captain make over his head. He feels his anger rise at the way he's being treated. *I might be a child, but it's still not right for them to ignore my choice. I don't want to stay on this ship if the Master isn't here. What would the point of that be? How can they ignore me like this when I'm standing right here?*

Viola leaves without a backward glance, a guide in attendance. It's like a dagger in his back. Pain squeezes his heart. His thoughts pour out the lifeblood of his soul. *Unfair. Cruel. Forsaken. Betrayed. Again, over and over again.* Another idea filters through the haze. *She is doing what she deems best—what she believes will keep me safe. But I don't want to be safe! I want to have this adventure. She can't decide for me!*

He senses heat rising within him—a hot air balloon

ready to explode. He's on the verge of running after Viola to offload all his resentment when a heavy hand settles on his shoulder. He looks up into the kind yet stern eyes of the captain. Smoky quartz beads, hard with determination, stare into him.

"It's not worth it, boy. Don't get mixed up in the inner politics of the imperial family. You're nothing but a fly in that game of leapfrog. You'll just end up as food for their intrigues. Be grateful for the opportunity she's given you. You have the ability to get out before it's too late, but as I said before, you're welcome to stay on this ship as long as you'd like, and you will have my protection."

Jo sucks air into his lungs. He clings to the fabric of his shirt in an attempt to control his rising anger. *Be polite. It doesn't matter what he thinks. I know what's right for me.* A second breath stills the tempestuous seas within him. Jo meets the captain's gaze and nods. "Thank you," he manages to push past his teeth. Then he pivots on his heel and strides out.

Once around the second corner, he takes a moment to gather his emotions. His intuition clamours for his attention. He has to speak with Viola and get her to understand this isn't the way forward for him. His future isn't on this ship, and he knows she will need his help to find her path towards forgiveness. He must make her understand that if she doesn't, the situation will drag her down the road back to everything she's spent her life running from. She'll just become like everyone else destroying all the worlds that make up the empire. *She needs to stay true to herself. I must fix this.*

He throws a quick prayer heavenwards before setting off at a trot. He doesn't know exactly where she's going, but he trusts in his need to find her. He opens up, stilling all the chatter in his mind. He wipes clean the slate within him, brushing away the feeling of resentment and replacing it with the still calm he associates with his god.

At the edges of his consciousness, he becomes aware of Viola's presence. He follows the tendrils his mind picks up and soon comes upon the attendant who led the storyteller away from the bridge. Jo bows his head to the man, who points to a door in the left wall. Before Jo can thank him, the man is gone.

Jo knocks. He hears a mumbled response and presses the surface in front of him. The door slides into the wall on his right with a soft hiss. He steps inside to find Viola spread-eagled on a large bed. It is about three times as wide as the bunk he sleeps on in the dorm. Off to the right are a leather armchair and a desk.

Viola only glances at him, then returns her gaze to the shiny white ceiling above her. Jo can sense her annoyance at being followed. Knowing he has to act fast to stop the spiral of her thoughts from sparking into anger, as it so often does, he steps forward in a bold motion.

"I have no intention of letting you give up on what you want. I—"

Before he can continue, she lets out a hollow laugh. "What I want? That is ashes now. Just go; leave me be."

"No." His brows draw together in frustration. She looks at him, but he doesn't let her speak. He charges on, unheeding of the disbelief he sees in her eyes. "You're being tested. Are you going to give in and give up now? Or are you willing to see things through, even when you don't know how what you want might come to pass? Trust in the process, Master. When we allow it to happen, the Mother-Father showers us in abundance. The Great Parent is on our side, but we have to trust."

Viola shakes her head. "I don't have the energy to listen to your nonsense anymore. It is over, boy. She won. She always knew she would, because she has all the resources at her disposal. I could never go against it, and finally, that is exactly what's coming to pass. My rebellion—my life—has been pointless. I failed. Life shows me at every turn that I cannot trust it. I should not expect anything because I shall always be disappointed."

Jo wants to cut in, but Viola raises a hand, silencing his impulsive desire to speak. "A cottage and a garden? That place for me to settle and tell my stories. It is a sick joke—even ridiculous. I shall never find peace. There is no point in expecting anything better from life. With everyone else being put in danger, I realise it is entirely futile to resist. If I keep chasing after the impossible dream, I shall just cause myself more pain. I have learned my lesson now; I cannot expect anything from life."

She dismisses him with a wave of her hand, but Jo ignores her. He closes his eyes, seeking the calm he needs to get through to her. *I have to make her see there is another way.* Viola's words echo in his mind. *I cannot expect anything from life.*

"Have you ever thought it might be life that's expecting something from you? You've just proven you know the difference between right and wrong. You won't sacrifice everyone on this ship for your gain. That's noble. It's in alignment with who you are. And still you believe you have to give it all up. What if this is a test? What if this is the last hurdle before you're given your perfect opportunity?"

Viola shakes her head, but Jo continues, his voice becoming louder, filling the room with his thoughts. "Right now, you feel helpless, but you also know, for this moment, your decision is the right one. Is there any difference in how you felt back then when you chose to leave your home? When you selected this path, how did you feel here?" He taps his right hand over his heart.

"I was completely divided," she replies. "I felt terrible —as if I was letting everyone down just to do what I wanted to. It was as though my desires and my duty were irreconcilable. I also felt I was a disappointment because my dream did not align with what they wanted."

Jo is silent, allowing her words to filter through to him, to settle in his mind. He senses her watching him and meets her gaze. "The Mother-Father doesn't want the children of this universe to experience disappointment or the sense we're letting someone down. That's why you're guided by a moral compass in the first place. Life breeds life. Your heart, your inner voice, can never lie to you. Do what you know is right—always."

"What is the point? It is hopeless anyway."

He cuts in, feeling his anger rising. "How much time and energy have you put into the thought that everything is pointless and that you can't have what you want? How long have you imagined *this* would happen?" He gestures in an all-encompassing circle. "How many times have you thought about this result?"

Viola sits up and meets his gaze squarely for the first time in the conversation. "I have always known it," she says, shrugging. "How long? I don't know."

"You said you've been on the run for twenty-eight years and that you've *always* known this would happen. Right?"

"Yes, precisely!"

"You've spent most days for the past 28 years dreaming of getting caught, worrying about failing and being dragged back against your will, kicking and screaming." She doesn't say anything, so he continues. "A few weeks ago, you thought of another possibility. How long have you considered that?"

She shrugs. "As you say, a few weeks."

"All day, every day?"

"Heavens, no! Maybe a few times a day. Sometimes not at all."

"And you're surprised that the Mother-Father hands you what you've poured energy into for twenty-eight years, even when that nightmare has been replaced with a new vision that you've only been working on for a few days?"

Viola remains silent.

The anger is subsiding, and his voice softens. "We're always granted what we wish for as long as we prove, through our behaviour, that we want to make it a reality. Our thoughts guide our actions, and those direct our outcomes. You left home with the fear of pursuit. Your fear became a reality, and your thoughts have fed your actions bringing you to this point—constantly foreseeing capture. When I left home, I feared I might die of starvation, or worse, all alone in the world, but I held that fear at bay by feeding my dream of becoming a storyteller and making that a possibility I could achieve. I recognised my fear for what it is—one option. I chose not to pursue it because it wasn't a result I wanted. I focused wholeheartedly on what I did want to experience." He pauses, gauging her reaction. Viola is still, absorbing his words.

Jo pulls the armchair about so it faces the bed and he settles into it. "Sometimes, what we wish for doesn't come to pass the way we hoped, but it always comes to pass. My people know this, although what happened with me and the prophecy made them waver in their belief. The Mother-Father reminded me this knowledge is part of the message my people bear. It is also the reason why we can do the things you deem impossible, like cleansing the blight. We know all things are possible as long as we believe. Now, if you accept that this is a test, what is your response to The Great Parent? Do you want this outcome, which is fuelled by years of fear and worrying, or do you want to insist on the shift you've begun? Are you willing to trust that your new vision is possible if you allow it to be?"

"Yes, but *how*?"

"When you ask how, you can only think from within your understanding in the now. That's why you need to relax your mind. You accept that every child can learn to speak, right? It is obvious, taken for granted, that all children will eventually learn to communicate through speech."

Another shrug is the only answer he receives.

"Do you need to know *how* each child learns to speak?"

Her brow wrinkles.

"That's not important because we know the child will learn, eventually, in its own way. We know it's possible because all other children that have gone before have achieved it. Do you agree?"

Viola nods. "Yes, I suppose so."

"Can you trust me when I say that knowing what one wants has worked for my people for thousands of years? That wishing in accordance to the deep desires of our hearts and staying true to ourselves and the good within us creates miraculous results? Can you let go of the how? Just because I know it works."

She swallows hard. He sees her fighting, but then her eyes soften. "Okay. I suppose I can trust you in that. You are saying I should end this now? I go back and face the music?"

"I'm not you. I don't hold your answers. What does your heart tell you?"

"Accepting this outcome feels difficult but right, somehow," she acknowledges.

"Then that's the sign; it's what you must do. Life isn't an abstract thing. It is tied to us—concretely. We do life's work. Sometimes we choose a different path; we fight against what is right for us because it's terrifying to do the difficult thing. We let our fear turn everything into Mshrali dust. When you give in to fear, you're simply allowing your situation to determine the results in your life, as though you have no power to influence what will happen. The thing is, you still get to choose. Do you follow your heart, even if it's hard to do, or do you give in to your fears? Are you satisfied with the result you're currently experiencing?"

"No, I am not."

Her voice is laced with irritation, and Jo matches her tone when he responds, "Then do something about it. Take responsibility for your life."

Viola chuckles suddenly, her voice taking on a wry tone. "That was a good one, Jo. You are right—you and your whopping thirteen years of wisdom. Now it is my turn to share something with you. I have kept it a secret, and it is time you know about it."

He blinks. *What is she talking about? There are other secrets?*

She seems to sense his confusion and smiles. "It is a good thing—I think." Her voice is soft.

His mind fires several hundred thoughts per second and he sits back in his chair when Viola gestures for calm.

Once he's settled, she says, "Tell me a story. Anything. Perhaps go for something you have worked on yourself. I know you have been working on your own things. It would be good for you to share something close to your heart, not a tale you have learned but some piece you created yourself."

Jo pushes back the thoughts tumbling through him, the questions that rail against this waste of time. The still voice of his intuition whispers that he should trust Viola. *This is important. Something I've worked on myself,* he muses. Then the penny drops and his anger and frustration at the situation channel into his intense passion for change. A poem he's spent hours refining becomes the wellspring from which words spill in a fluid waterfall.

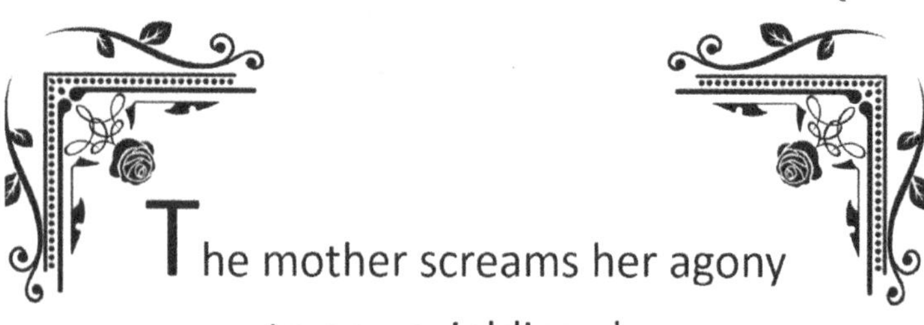

The mother screams her agony
to an unyielding sky.
Her children rend her rocky
entrails,
Uncaring.
The mother cries for her children
As they poison her life's essence,
Unheeding.

The father shouts his anger to an
unyielding sky.
His children chain him where he
stands,
Uncaring.
The father cries out to warn his
children
As they gut his legacy,
Unheeding.

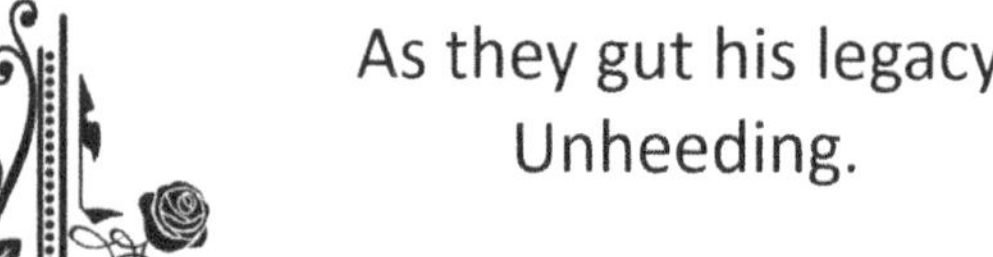

The children hear nothing,
They listen only to the sound of
the treasures they seek.
The children see nothing,
Their eyes are open only to the
wealth they desire.
The children feel nothing,
Their hearts only beat for the
prizes they covet.

More, more, more
Now, now, now
The tempo of the tantrum, ever-
increasing.
More, more, more
Now, now, now
Insatiable desire leaves only
room for the self.
More, more, more
Now, now, now

Paradise lies just ahead!

STOP,
I say.
Cease this madness!
Stop.
Unshackle your hearts, unblind
your eyes,

See the darkness that weaves
through all you do.
Paradise cannot be found on a
path of shadows.
Cease your incessant grabbing,
With greed clouding all that is.
Your desires leave chaos in their
wake!
Disdain is the hallmark of this era.

STOP,
I say.
Cease this madness!
Stop.
Unshackle your hearts, unblind
your eyes,

Return the life-blood to
Your mother.
Unbind the shackles from
Your father.

Give voice to the life you have
denied.
Give life to the world you plunder.

Look around at the destruction,
Despair is nigh.

But you are hope.
You can see.
You glimpse eternity.

Look around,
You can forge great wings,
With your words, deeds and
other things.

I say stop,
Breathe,
Think,
Dream.
Be your paradise.
Now.

Jo is pulled along on the passion of his desire for change. He is so occupied by the words, by the meaning of his message, that he doesn't notice something else happening while he speaks. It is only when the last word rings out that his attention falls on shimmering waves of undulating light flowing from him. He is surrounded by soft sheets of colour, constantly changing, gleaming around him.

His mouth hangs open. *What is this?*

"I have been covering it up ever since the first time you told me a story. I was afraid if others saw this, they would start asking very difficult questions. I have never seen anything like it." Her voice is tender, husky even.

Jo watches the glimmers of light fade into the air. He blinks. "What is it?" His voice trembles and he realizes he's standing.

"I don't know. As I said, I have never come across anything of this sort. Although, I can hazard a guess that it is the expression of your unique magic, whatever it is that the holy man of your people saw when you were conceived. Again, I do not know how such a thing is possible since magic is the province of human women, but perhaps there is some secret lineage you do not know anything about. You may have some elven blood in you." She nods in response to his widening eyes. "Yes, yes. I know the elves became extinct centuries ago, but as creatures of pure magic, they were renowned for their universal ability to wield power."

Jo feels his legs shaking. His body is hot and cold at the same time. *Magic? Can such a thing be possible?* His knees give way from under him, and he crumples to the ground. *Can it really be true?*

Tears, like silver sparkles, gather in his eyes. In part, it's the pain in his constricting chest that calls them forth, but more than anything, it's his sense of gratitude. As his relief courses down his cheeks, his eyes lift, looking past the sterile severity of the cabin ceiling and searching into the great beyond, far removed from where he kneels. *Thank you!*

He's brought back to the moment by Viola's arms folding him into an embrace. She pulls him against her and rests his head on a shoulder.

"I'm not a failure?" he whispers, disbelief still haunting his voice. Years of torment, his sister's taunts, and the silent disillusionment reflected in his father's eyes—all dissipate. They were the last doubt weighing down his heart, holding him back even when the truth of his intuition whispered that their viewpoint was false. He'd never dared believe it before this moment.

"No, my dear boy. You have never been a disappointment."

"But how?"

She snorts. "Wasn't it you who just told me that the how isn't important."

He laughs, pulling away from her embrace. He sees drops glistening in the corners of her eyes.

"Your magic rests in your ability to tell stories. I began to understand the extent of it in Ilwych when your deep desire for cleanliness was transferred onto those who heard you speak—first in the market and then later at the tavern as well. Who knows what you achieved at the merchants' guild."

Her smile is broad, and he laughs again, buoyed on elation. He recalls the beauty of the magic, how the undulating light filled the whole room. He brushes a hand over his face and takes a breath. "What do I do now?" he wonders.

"I know a fantastic musician in Téarman. Since we are stopping, you can take a recommendation from me and go to visit him. That poem you just offered was ten times more powerful than anything I have tried to keep under wraps with your prose. There was no way my limited power could have contained you today. I think you need to learn the craft of a bard. That will increase your reach. After that, your guess is as good as mine."

Jo glances down at his arms in wonder. It is a lot for him to take in. His tongue flicks over his lips. They tremble with the tumult of his emotions. *Should I try again?* he wonders.

Viola forestalls him. "Jo, I think it will be best if you learn to contain the visible manifestation. Until you know more about what you can do, it may be best to keep it quiet. There is no knowing what others might do."

He nods, a smile now twitching at his lips. A fire ignites within him, excitement mixed with the desire to learn. "Can you teach me this now, Master?"

"I do not know if my techniques will work for you, but the basic idea is to hold in your head the image of what you want others to see. Do you remember the glamour I used when we arrived in Ilwych?"

He nods, and she continues. "When you are telling stories or performing in any way, you should focus on an image of yourself without the signs of magic. I do not know if it will work for you, though."

Chapter Eighteen

Viola sits at the captain's desk in one corner of the spacious cabin and speaks into a small device. Her tone is measured. She glances over at the leather armchair where her apprentice sleeps, a soft snore escaping his parted lips. When she finishes her recorded recommendation to her friend Cerddor, she observes Jo for a moment. Her mind wanders over the coincidence of their meeting and the time spent travelling together, and gratitude fills her heart. She soars on the wings of all she's learned since she met this unassuming boy from a community that rejected him.

Her buoyancy reverses, and the weight of such tragedies pulls her down again. Viola remembers her mother's dismissal and the long years of being hounded because she stubbornly refused to do as she was told. *Funny how my mother chose the wrong tactic to keep me there and has since spent all this time and these resources trying to bring me back. The world works in mysterious ways. Perhaps this boy is right.* "Jo," she muses aloud.

She wonders what his renounced name is as she brings a hand to her brow. It doesn't matter. Jo is as good a name as any, and it suits him. She is glad she met him because it's made her living nightmare seem less awful. *Perhaps it was meant to be, as he says. There are no coincidences.* She thinks about it. It is such a strange notion to consider she was meant to be on the run for twenty-eight years, just to be captured and taken back. Why are they still chasing her? It's not like they can marry her off like they intended to when she was in her twenties. *I am too old now, past my child-bearing years. Knowing mother, it is just a matter of proving a point.*

She shifts. Her mind turns towards the future. *What will become of me? And what of that cottage and the dog? Is peace of mind even possible under these circumstances? Is all of that still an option, as he suggests?* His words echo in her mind, a bubble rising to the surface of her consciousness. *It isn't about denying the conditions but about denying their power to rule your life.* Viola glances over at the sleeping figure in the armchair. She stands and crosses the room to him, pulling a spare blanket off the end of the bed as she passes by. She drapes the cover over him, gently folding the edges around his sleeping form. Her heart swells at the sight of his peaceful expression.

The hollowness of loss creeps into her aching bones. *I never wanted to give this up.* She takes in the sight of him, tousled hair flopped over his brows, his eyelashes resting on his cheekbones, which are far less prominent now than when she first met him. *Why could they not leave me to do things my way, instead of insisting on taking control of my life and dictating everything? I could have had both, and they could have had their heir.*

She turns sharply, a sigh parting her lips as she strides to the bed. *No matter. That opportunity is gone. At least I could have this moment with Jo.* "Dear, sweet boy," she murmurs as she once more glances over towards him. "We are a pair, aren't we? You without a mother and me with my tales and nothing else." She lies down, staring up at the ceiling as she thinks. *Tales that make the world a better place, deliberately fostering a shift in how people see the world and how they treat it, now that is something I could get behind—a nice addition to this impossible dream.* "Ha, I did it again," she murmurs, watching as Jo sleeps; he is a picture of serenity. *He would tell me to keep believing, even when all reason dictates it should be futile. I shall go with improbable but not impossible.*

"All hands prepare for landing. Passengers, follow safety procedures," blares a voice through the ship. Viola sits up straight, disoriented. She glances about her, struggling to remember where she is. Then the memories of the previous day crash over her in an overwhelming wave. She glances at the armchair. It is empty except for a neatly folded blanket.

"All hands prepare for landing. Passengers, follow safety procedures," the announcement repeats.

Viola settles back onto the bed and finds the safety button beside her right hand. She wriggles into a comfortable position, pulls the broad safety belt across her torso and presses the bright green pulsating light. The transparent bubble snaps into place above her, cocooning her with its g-force-reducing tech.

"Landing procedures in progress. Passengers, follow safety procedures."

The steady hum of the engines changes to a whine and a powerful force pulls at Viola. She remembers stories of how it was in the past, before the safety bubble was developed, how the body suffered during entry to a planet's surface. She closes her eyes and tries to fade out the intensity of the experience while thinking about what will happen once she disembarks. After a while, the rattling and jerking motions subside, and stillness fills the giant machine. She presses the button once more, and the transparent bubble shifts and stows. She listens to the silence. Her ears strain after the interminable days spent hearing past the continuous hum of the engines. The stillness is absolute.

She swings her legs over the side but stays seated. *No point getting ahead of myself and showing my agitation. Better to act cool and see if I can use the situation to my advantage. Who knows what opportunity might present itself?*

A few minutes later, that resolve lies discarded at the back of her mind while she paces back and forth through the cabin. She is overwhelmed by her agitation. Sitting still, being the image of collected calm; this just isn't who she is. She berates herself, thinking about all the rigorous training of her upbringing and how little she retained it over the years. *I never wanted any of it,* she thinks. *I left because that wasn't a life I wanted. And my choice gave me a life I enjoyed even less.*

She wonders where they are and why she always has to wait on others. In contrast, what was nice about travelling on her own was she didn't need to answer to anyone else. *Patience,* chimes in another part of her. *Patience? Bah!* Her anxious self replies. *Never been patient. Not going to learn it now.*

Her brows are tugged into a decisive v-shape as she paces a crescent through the room. All the while, her thoughts bombard her with worries and what-ifs. Her breathing becomes fast and shallow, but she pays no mind to it.

In mid-stride, Viola hears the soft hiss of the door. She finds herself face to face with the captain.

"Ah, good," he exclaims. "They're ready for you, Lady."

Viola nods. "Could you see Jo gets this pack?" she asks, gesturing to her backpack in the corner of the room. "I shan't be needing it now."

"Certainly, Lady. I'll see he gets your belongings."

She steadies herself with an inhale and gestures that he should lead the way. As they near the docking gate, Viola wonders what will become of Jo. She glances about, hoping to catch sight of him, realising she never bade him farewell. At the exit, ready to see her off, are many of the passengers she got to know in her moments of high spirits, but Viola can't see the one face she's looking for. The captain bows to her and steps aside, gesturing for her to proceed alone.

As she steps out onto the gangplank and into the blinding light of the outdoors, she thinks, *At least I had the opportunity to show him he isn't a failure at all. That gift is greater than anything else; I am blessed to have seen the extent of his very beautiful magic.*

In the next moment, all thought is wiped from her mind. A wall of hot, humid air encases her, making it hard to breathe. A searing yellow sun pounds onto the open expanse where the spaceship is docked. Incandescent waves bounce from the sheer metal hull onto the smooth surface beneath her feet and reflect back into the air, suffocating her with unbearable heat.

Viola shields her eyes from the glare, brushing away the beads of sweat pearling on her brow. When her eyes adjust to the brightness of the environment, she makes out a group of people standing at the entrance of an extravagant building. The grand lines of the edifice swoop and whirl in ostentatious architectural designs constructed from unfamiliar, sandy brown rock. A series of tall glass windows break the monotony of the stone surface.

Her attention is drawn to the figures waiting to greet her. A snort of derision escapes her at the sight of their outfits. The woman standing at the head of the delegation is dressed in orange so garish that Viola wants to shade her eyes from it. She senses a shudder threatening to tear through her. It hovers at the base of her skull, and she bites down hard, grinding her teeth to prevent herself from showing obvious signs of revulsion.

How can anyone willingly wear something like that? I forgot how ridiculous the citizens of Baile can be when it comes to fashion. They have no conception of what is flattering on the human form.

Her judgement bears down on her mind. She tries to draw her gaze away from the woman's exposed flesh, only to find herself faced with a visage plastered with paint several millimetres thick. Her eyes brush over to the next person, and then she wishes she hadn't let them. The man's face is equally painted, and his cleanly-shaven chest gleams in the sunlight.

The party bows, and the woman in orange smiles. Viola feels sick to her stomach at the sight.

"Welcome to the city of Baile, My Lady."

The voice reminds Viola of overly sweetened juice. It tickles at her memory, but Viola brushes the thought away with a grimace and snaps, "Just get on with it."

Chapter Nineteen

Jo tosses and turns in his sleep. He cries out and sits up, knocking his head against the berth above him. Rubbing his head, he glances about, getting his bearings. He is dazed and bleary-eyed, but he notices there's no one else in the room. Last he remembers, he returned to his berth for landing and it was full with all the crew. He's on his own. Then the silence hits him. After weeks of hearing the constant hum of running engines, the stillness is eerie.

He jumps from the bed, landing in a flat-out run. He winds through the passageways, his mind racing because he realises he just had a vision. Something about the re-entry into planetary atmosphere must have put him into a trance. The halls are deserted. In response, his forehead twitches into a series of furrows. Coming around a corner, he charges headlong into the first mate.

Trying to keep his balance, Jo gasps an apology. A string of curses is all the answer he gets.

The first mate makes to walk around Jo, so he flings his arms wide and stammers, "My master—where is she?"

The well-built man's round face darkens into a scowl. He looks down his nose at Jo and tries to shove him aside. "Out of my way, boy."

Jo doesn't move. He rephrases his question instead. "The storyteller, where is she? I must speak with her."

The look of disdain in the man's face deepens. "The highborn lady left the ship as soon as we arrived and is in the safe custody of Téarman's senate in Baile."

Jo's heart was already pounding in his throat, but now the realisation that he missed her, that he didn't get to say goodbye, tightens iron bands across his chest. He gasps for air. Spots dance across his vision. Anguish tears through him when the memory of the vision, his dream, paints a pristine image in his mind.

The first mate jostles him, bringing him back from the brink of despair. Before the man can take two steps, Jo blocks him off again. "Please, where's the captain?" He is frantic now.

"The captain has no time for the likes of you. Now, be gone! I have business to attend to."

Urgency turns to anger, and Jo demands, "Where's the captain?"

The man ignores him and walks off. Jo is about to run

after him again when he realises something. He is aware of the captain's whereabouts. Somehow, he knows exactly where he'll find the man. Shaking his head to clear away the questions that tumble over one another, trying to grab his attention, Jo rushes through the grid of intersecting hallways. Like a bloodhound following a scent, he trails the hunch that leads him ever onwards. While his feet slap out a rhythm on the smooth floor of the vessel, his mind goes over the details of his dream.

The captain is in his quarters and Jo barges in without knocking. He sees the big man sitting at a desk, leaning forward, one elbow propped on the surface in front of him, the other meaty hand hovering by his mouth. He is muttering into a device. Jo comes to a halt, suddenly realising he's broken all protocol. This is reinforced by the man's stern gaze, which pierces Jo from above the wild forest of his beard.

"I'm sorry, Captain," he mumbles while trying to catch his breath. "I'd like to get a message to my Master. Can you please help me?"

"Any one of the ship's attendants can provide you with a device. It's just a matter of recording your message."

Jo shakes his head. "No, sir. This message has to be written on paper."

The captain's brow crinkles into a series of ridges and valleys, emphasising his balding pate, usually hidden under a navy cap. Silence draws out between them. Then the man sighs and opens a drawer. He pulls out a sheaf of paper and plucks a pen from the darkened recess, holding them out towards the boy, who shakes his head once more.

"I can't write, Captain." His voice is a hoarse whisper. He feels ashamed. This is a serious failing; he knows it. Everyone in the empire knows how to read and write—everyone except him. Jo feels heat rising to his ears in response to the captain's expression of shocked disbelief.

Squirming on the spot, Jo whispers, "Can you please write it for me?"

Shifting in his seat, the older man places the paper on the desk, the pen almost disappearing between his fingers, and asks, "What'll it be then, boy?"

Jo dictates the two lines he wants to convey. While the captain folds the paper, Jo asks, "Can you help me to get a speaking engagement here in this city?

"You'd better not start any trouble, boy. Especially not for the lady. She's had enough difficulties as it is."

"I just want to tell a story," he mumbles in reply.

Hard brown eyes appraise him once more. Then the man rises and walks over to where Jo stands. He settles a hand on Jo's shoulder; it's warm, and there's kindness in his eyes.

"I can see you're trying to help her. Whatever it is you plan to do, just make sure you don't get caught. That could make things very difficult for her, and undoubtedly, it would also be a bad thing for you. There are consequences for meddling with the imperials."

"I don't care about *them*," Jo mutters. "She doesn't want to go back in this way. I want her to be able to do it with dignity."

"We're all worthy of being treated with dignity. I can agree with you on that." His massive hand comes down on Jo's shoulder three times, jostling the boy. The captain grabs his hat and heads to the exit. He turns in the doorway, saying, "I'll get this delivered to her, discreetly." He gestures with the note. "I'll also let you know if and when you'll be speaking. That may take a few days." Jo nods, following the captain to the door. Then the man turns as if struck by a sudden thought. "She left you all her belongings. The backpack there is yours," and he points towards it.

Jo glances at the bag leaning against the wall of the cabin. By the time he rounds the door, calling out, "Thank you, Captain!" the man is already at the next corner but raises a hand in acknowledgement just before he turns out of sight.

Jo spends three days in an agitated state. Most of the passengers are away on land, along with many of the crew. Jo doesn't want to leave the ship. He knows the captain could send for him at any time and he wants to be close by.

Besides, he keeps telling himself, *I'm going to be staying on this planet, so I'll get an opportunity to explore and see the sights when I make the journey to see the musician Master recommended.*

He spends most of his time thinking about the dream he had—a message from the Mother-Father; he is certain of it. Jo also goes over the details of a plan that has been formulating in his mind since the moment he woke up. Pacing back and forth in the deserted entertainment area, Jo comes to a sudden stop when he sees the first mate striding towards him.

The man looks irritable. "Captain sends for you, boy."

Jo brightens. "Thank you!" he exclaims as he rushes past.

The crowd waiting to hear him is enormous. Jo gazes over the sea of faces and feels his stomach flip-flop inside him. He's never seen so many people before. Their clothing seems odd; the colours are bright and vibrant, unusual to eyes that are used to greys and browns. The style is also markedly different from what he knows from his home planet, Mshrali. Here, showing off skin doesn't seem to be a problem, and he is drawn to the diversity of shades represented; there are so many variations of brown that he can't begin to find words for all of them.

His mind is also bombarding him with terms for all the other new things he's seeing. Once more, his brain somehow knows these words. *I should have gone out before. I know this happens when I come to new places, so why didn't I think to get it out of the way?*

He drops his gaze to the toes of his boots. They're bright and new; Viola bought them for him at the ship's cobbler. *I can't fail now. I know the Great Parent is with me and that I must succeed for the Master's sake.* He knows this is so much bigger than he is.

Jo draws himself up to his full height. He hears soft giggles rippling through the crowd. Whispers swing back and forth like a wind rustling through a forest. Clenching all his courage into his fists, Jo steps out onto the stage and into full view of the crowd.

The level of noise increases as the speculation of the gathered assembly grows. Jo ignores them. He glances up into the bright blue sky above him and launches into his tale. Within moments, the people cease their whispering as they fall under the spell of his voice. By the time the waving tendrils of his magic escape his rudimentary attempt to keep them in check, most of his listeners are so engrossed in the tale that they don't even notice the dance of colourful lights that plays around him.

As the words of *The Companion's Tale* pour from him, he steps out of himself, reliving the vision from his dream. This is the exact moment he was shown, and he knows all will unfold as it should.

Chapter Twenty

Viola spends most of her days in the rooms she's been given. They're sumptuous, a vivid reminder of what she once called home. The light drapes billowing on a gentle breeze, and the dimness of the rooms that keeps the heat at bay—both pull her thoughts down the winding passages of the past.

A timid knock brings Viola out of her reverie. "Enter," she calls.

The door swings open, but nothing happens. Viola rolls over on the bed to see what's going on. Bright green fabric brings out the pale shade of wide eyes in a delicate face. The girl carries a bowl which is heaped with an assortment of delectable fruits.

The sight of the trembling figure in the doorway is a reminder of Jo. Viola's memory superimposes his half-starved form, as it was when she first met him, on the scene before her. She shakes her head to dismiss the image and, although her heart goes out to this frightened child, Viola remains where she is. She has a part to play in the manoeuvrings of her extended family, and she won't show any of her cards. Keeping up her guise of irascible old woman, Viola jerks her head towards a corner where a low table is accompanied by two reclining couches with fine upholstery.

The girl carries the dish over and sets it down with a clatter. Some of the fruit spills from the sides and the child lets out a whimper.

Viola turns away and says as mildly as she dares, "Go."

Viola watches from the corner of her eye as the trembling figure stumbles out of the room and a guard closes the door behind her. Viola sighs. *Escape is not an option.* She looks at the bunch of juicy purple anggur that tumbled onto the table. They look delicious, but Viola doesn't know if she can trust such things. *Would anyone be interested in poisoning me? To stop me from going back?* Knowing her family, Viola decides not to take the risk.

Then something else catches her attention. A pale cream corner peeks out from beneath the fruit. She draws nearer and makes out a small square of paper wedged under a golden nanas. She realises that if the girl hadn't dropped them, it would have been completely hidden by the anggur.

Viola glances around her, a nervous action honed by

years on the run. She slips the paper out of the bowl while pretending to decide what to eat. Turning, she slumps on the bed again and tosses back onto the table the one anggur she did pick up. It rolls off, coming to a stop on the polished wooden flooring.

Keeping her curiosity at bay, Viola closes her eyes again and pretends to drift off to sleep. She hopes they only have humans watching her. If drones or other mechanical wonders are involved, then she knows all her posturing is pointless. Still, she pretends to go to sleep. After waiting as long as she can bear, Viola opens her fist and unfolds the paper. The two lines bring a smile to her lips.

"Master, I had a dream. Trust in the possibility of dreams. I'm determined to tell a story to the people of Baile. Don't accept the invitation to join."

She reads the note a second time, then holds it between two fingers, shuts her eyes tight and purses her lips. With a hiss, it evaporates, leaving nothing more than the smell of singed paper hanging in the air. *I hope that was little enough. Would not do for them to be able to trace the spark.*

What is that boy planning? Viola wonders. She knows it has to do with what they spoke about during their time spent on the spaceship. *Trust in the possibility of dreams*, she muses. Her mind calls up the image of a cottage, overgrown with ivy on one wall and with flowers adding splashes of colour in beds laid out around the building. A low brick wall borders a patch of green grass, and large flagstones lead through a wrought-iron gate onto a lane. *I cannot create it right now, but I can make it welcome,* she thinks.

Calm infuses Viola as she dreams of a life living in harmony with her purpose as a storyteller, but where she can also stay in one place. She sees herself sitting at a window, her fingers flying over the keys as she records new tales onto a device. Real books line the inside of the cottage. *Ah,* she muses, *what I would give to smell a dusty old-fashioned tome!*

Every evening, Viola is invited to dine with the Baile elite and every day she declines to do so. After receiving the note from Jo, she is surprised when the ambassador, who met her at the ship, calls upon her.

"My Lady, Isperia," the woman greets Viola.

Shuddering inwardly, Viola takes in the woman's lime-green outfit with its billowing trousers and tight-fitting strapless top. "Cousin," she replies.

"Ah, so you did recognise me?"

"It is hard under all that paint you wear, but your voice is still the same. Then again, you were always eccentric, so it is no surprise you fit right in here on Téarman."

Brown eyes darken and narrow to slits. "Do not even dare, Isperia. You cannot begin to understand what it is like to be relegated to a place like this."

Viola's lips draw into a thin smile. "Oh, Natesari, believe me when I say, you could do worse. What did you do to displease her and get yourself assigned to this dump?"

The other woman's hands ball into fists. Her jaw clenches and Viola hears teeth grating against each other. "Clearly something stupid," Viola adds, cocking her head to the side. She leans back, flicking her hand in disinterest. "Well, do not think handing me over to her will make any difference. I doubt I shall be your ticket back into Her Grace's good opinion."

Natesari's eyes light up. "I would not be so sure of that," she smiles wickedly. "Your return is a matter of principle, and all of us know how much you are coveted. She's practically emptied the coffers for your sake."

Viola lies back, closing her eyes and pretending indifference. *If that were true, they would have caught me before now.*

"Would you honour all of us Baileans and deign to dine in company tonight?" Natesari's tone shifts, sweet fruits glazed in honey.

Viola shakes her head, cracking an eye open to

observe the response. Her cousin's fuchsia lips purse into a thin line, but the ambassador bows her head, accepting Viola's decision. "Oh yes," she adds with a laugh, "I heard your *apprentice* will be making an appearance tomorrow. Will you join us for that? It must be such fun to train another in one's profession. You should be proud he is permitted to speak, for I hear he is of very lowly birth."

Holding onto her show of nonchalance, Viola suppresses the outburst desperate to escape her at Natesari's emphasis and the disdain harboured in her voice. Viola holds back the tirade, only narrowing her eyes to show her displeasure, and mutters, "What my one-time apprentice does is no concern of mine. You are welcome to tell me what you think of his performance, but I have no interest in the trifles of the life I leave behind. Thank you, but no."

Her cousin bristles and flounces out of the room. Once the door closes behind her, Viola murmurs to herself, "No, madam ambassador, I have no interest in giving you any more power than you already have here. I shall not elevate you by association in the eyes of the people in Baile." Her thoughts drift to Jo. Will he survive among this pack of serigala? She knows they could tear him apart with their political scheming, and wonders if she did the right thing leaving him behind. She takes a deep breath, acknowledging to herself that it was the best she could do. *He has proven himself hardy, and he clearly has something up his sleeve. I shall just have to trust he will get through this.*

The next day, Viola reclines on one of the chairs in her room. A ripple of energy courses through the air, raising the hairs on her arms. In her mind, she hears Jo's voice whisper. *I'm determined to tell a story*. In a heartbeat, Viola comes to her feet and glances out of the window.

The courtyard below her is deserted. *Trust in the possibility of dreams.* She leans out over the railing and sees she can jump down to the level below. She hesitates, then a part of her cries out, *Just do it!*

She jumps.

Her landing is hard and jars her knees. She gasps as she stretches her legs out again. *I am too old for this.* She snaps back with a withering retort, *Old or not, I do not want to stick around to be their bargaining chip. Maybe the boy's distraction will work, and I can find a way out of here.*

She stands in a tiled courtyard with pot plants lining the walls. Bright tropical flowers bloom from the dark green. It is mid-afternoon, and the heat is sticky and oppressive; sweat trickles down her face. To Viola's left, the courtyard leads into a tunnel under the building, and she makes out deep leafy green beyond. To her right, she spies a door leading inside.

Seeing no other obvious way out of the courtyard, Viola heads through the tunnel and into a rainforest garden. The smell of damp earth tingles in her senses as her eyes travel up and up the tall stem of a palm. Ahead of her, a paved walkway that leads into silent, cool shade is lined by leafy fronds in varying shades of green with streaks of yellow or red. Dabs of pink and orange blossoms bring the verdure to life with colour.

Viola follows the path, now and then checking over her shoulder to make sure she is alone. The gentlest breath of wind is the only companion she has as she traverses the refreshing tropical glade, rustling the leaves of the otherwise tranquil garden.

Soon, the path curves to the right. She pauses to appraise the situation, then pushes through the undergrowth ahead of her. Within moments, she comes to a wall almost twice her height. She glances to either side and sees one palm tree that's close enough to help her scale the barrier.

It doesn't take her long to reach the tree and attempt climbing it, but the fibrous palm bark is mostly smooth, with few supports that could serve as toe and hand-holds. She swears under her breath and looks about her again. This tree is the best option she has, so taking a deep breath, she steps up once more and tries again. A furrow of determination forms between her eyes as she thinks to herself, *I shall succeed—somehow.*

A few failed attempts later, she finds a crack in the wall that she can use for support, and with one great heave, she's sitting atop the barrier. She pauses a moment to catch her breath before taking stock of her situation. The wall is wide enough to walk on and beyond it spreads a city of haphazard differently-coloured buildings. In the distance, she sees the grey shadow of a wall circling the dilapidated mess of the city.

Looks like baby brother's playpen, she thinks. A giggle escapes her. A cool breeze caresses her cheeks, and she glances up. The intensity of the sky softens with gathering clouds, a promise of reprieve from the heat. Her gaze drifts from the heavens to a road surface below. The sheer drop facing her is daunting.

Vertigo assails her, forcing her to shut her eyes and trust the solid rock beneath her. *I need a rope*, she thinks. Something tickles her shoulder. She looks around to see long-fingered palm fronds dancing in the wind. She glances from the flexible palm leaf to the ground.

It might just work. She appraises the distance to the ground once more and looks back at the makeshift rope she was given. *No time to dilly-dally; I am just going to have to go with it and hope for the best.*

Viola grabs hold of the stem at a point where it's thick enough to grasp properly. She swings a leg over the edge of the wall, then thinks better of it and turns around, supporting herself with one hand while keeping the other on the palm leaf. She stretches her feet, easing herself over the rim and pressing the toes of her soft slippers into the hard surface of the wall. There's no purchase, and she kicks off the lightweight shoes which tumble to the ground below.

Feeling gravity drag at her body, Viola grasps the palm with her free hand and gives herself over to nature. She plummets groundwards; then her arms jerk as the palm leaf strains against its anchorage at the base of the tree stem. Her shoulder bumps against the wall, and she grazes her wrist. Ignoring the sting, she clings to the palm and looks down. She is still a fair distance from the ground, but close enough to jump.

She is about to let go of the leaf when a tearing sound emanates from above her and the frond comes free. Viola crumples into a heap on the hard surface of the road below, knocking a knee numb, followed by intense tingling. She takes a moment to steady herself and catch her breath. Her feet burn against the hot surface of the road, and she casts about for her shoes. She slips them on, then grabs the palm frond and places it in what she hopes is a natural position. *Let us hope they think it came off by itself and do not realise I have left the premises.*

She dashes into an alley heading in the direction of the city wall she saw from above. It dawns on her how deserted the city is; even when she sat atop the wall, she couldn't make out any people. The afternoon is so still it makes her uneasy. Keeping to the shadows, she darts forward, pausing for apprehensive moments during which she glances about. Block by block she makes her way through the empty streets.

Wiping her hands on her trousers, she realises that streaks of green and brown mar the pristine whiteness of her outfit. Viola stops. *White.* She groans as the thought flits through her mind. Imperial white—like a beacon that she doesn't belong out there. Her heart beats in her throat, and a cold shiver runs up her spine. *Damn them and all their symbolic posturing. Curse the whole imperial enterprise.*

Fear extends its grasping claws towards her, but Viola dispels it by pursing her lips with determination. *None of that. I still have some tricks up my sleeve.* She weaves her fingers in the air around her, hoping there's enough time for the spark to dissipate so no one can trace what she's doing. With satisfaction, she watches a ripple spread about her frame and then she appears to be clothed more adequately for travelling. Sturdy brown trousers are matched with a simple grey blouse. She strides forward, hoping that the illusion will be enough to throw off the scent anyone who might be following her.

It takes her the better part of an hour to cross the deserted city. Even approaching the outskirts, she barely meets anyone. There are a few urchins who loiter in a blind alley, and she feels their eyes on her as she passes it by. Wondering what could be the reason for the lifelessness in Baile, Viola jumps in surprise at the rumble that emanates from the sky above.

In the next instant, the heavens tear open in a downpour that in a matter of seconds has Viola soaked to the bone. She tries to find shelter under the eaves of the nearest building, but it's pointless. Raindrops hit the ground so hard they splash up onto her legs. Moments later, the tropical rain passes and quiet returns to the street. The only sound comes from the brown stream that now courses over the cobbles.

Viola weaves her fingers through the air once more, tightening the illusion to make her appear dry, and then squelches along a raised sidewalk, dripping as she goes. *What a relief that everything is so wet. No one will notice my shoes squelching under the illusion.* She dismisses masking the sound, which would sap more of her energy and she is thankful she's been eating well of late, meaning the magic shouldn't drain her too much.

She comes out of the alley and onto a broad road that appears to cut through the city towards the outer gate. Water is still bubbling along the side of the street as Viola heads in the direction of the city wall. People are starting to crowd the sidewalks around her and insight sparks. *They were having an afternoon rest in the heat of the day and waiting for the downpour to come and go.* She is relieved that the customs of the place may aid her escape; no one was outdoors to see her leave the diplomatic precinct, and now she is simply one person in the crowd.

Soon after, Viola spies the gates. Four guards stand around, looking important, and she sees another two in a small gatehouse built onto the inner wall. She pauses and gathers her courage. Then she strides forward and out of the city with a single thought hovering in her mind: *That was too easy*.

Chapter Twenty-One

Jo's voice stills. He blinks, coming out of the trance of his tale. He stretches and smiles, knowing he has achieved something great. A ripple goes through the crowd that blankets the square before him. Then the silence splits in a roar of cheers and exuberant clapping. High-pitched whistles stab the tumultuous roar of approval and Jo bows. He makes eye contact with a group of finely dressed patrons on a balcony.

One of the women raises her hand, and silence engulfs the crowd once more. Her voice is high but carries powerfully throughout the open plaza, and Jo wonders what magical device she uses to be heard so clearly.

"Good people of Baile, we are pleased this itinerant storyteller has entertained you. His tale was charming. Shall we invite him to stay?" Her words are met with shouts and applause. She turns her attention to Jo. "Young man, I would like to extend you an invitation to stay here, in Baile, as my honoured guest."

Jo bows, taking the moment to think how best to respond. When he has straightened, he smiles. His voice carries on its own, without any external help. "I thank you and all the kind people of Baile for this great honour. However, I have not yet completed my training and wish to improve my skills. In accordance with my Master's wishes, I am expected by the mentor she has engaged. Master Cerddor lives in Abhainn, and I look forward to experiencing more of this wondrous country that is so different from my home. I will be glad to accept your hospitality should my path bring me back to Baile."

The woman's dark brows draw together, but she brushes over her irritation, saying, "As you wish. We shall see to it that you have an escort."

Jo swallows. He knows he can't refuse her a second time, so mumbles, "You are too kind." He pauses before adding, "Thank you."

He turns to walk from the stage and is met by two men. They're tall, dressed in tight trousers of bright red, bare chests gleaming bronze in the hot afternoon. One of them wears his ebony hair in a topknot with the sides shaved into whorls. The other has short dark brown hair and sports a trimmed beard. Jo's heart palpitates in an anguished thrum at the sight of two thin rods that hang from a strap over the shoulders of each. The words *taser* and *truncheon* flit through his mind and every cell in his body quivers. *Better watch myself around those two.*

His mouth is dry, and his nervous tongue twitches over his lips, but to no avail. He clears his throat and rasps, "Lead me where you must."

The first man inclines his head in a sharp motion and turns. Jo falls into step behind him with the other man following. Another shiver runs through him. His mind leaps through a series of possibilities, and he tries unsuccessfully to calm his jumpy nerves. He can't avoid seeing the rippling muscles and the liquid motion of the man ahead of him and how he places each step with harsh precision.

They lead him into a building with a polished floor and sweeping walls. Light streams in through partitions of different coloured glass, creating a playful pattern at Jo's feet. The air inside is cool in comparison to the sweltering clamminess outdoors. He follows his guard up a wide staircase of glistening marble.

Turning a corner, Jo stops short. He finds himself in a glassed-in corridor suspended above the crowd whom he entertained a little while earlier. The bridge leads from one building to another, but he feels as if he's floating above the sea of spectators who are pushing through the few exits to the plaza—ants, spilling out to go about their business.

"Ahem." The guard behind him clears his throat.

Jo stammers an apology, running after the other guard who stands at the exit of the bridge. His foot is tapping, the only indication of irritation. *They're put out at having been assigned to me,* he realises. *I must do my best to keep on their good side.*

The next building is even grander. Etchings run through the coloured glass, spilling images onto the floor where he walks. He tries to make sense of the scenes, but they're strangely warped by darker veins that swirl through the rainbow patches. The walls, too, are brightly painted. Some of the scenes he recognises from the tales he's learned from Viola—important moments in the history of the empire—but others are more obscure. An imperious voice jerks Jo from his thoughts.

"Ah, you are admiring the art." Up close, the woman who addressed him after his stint on-stage gives him the shivers. Her saffron outfit is sausage-casing tight, her bosom squeezed to the point that it seems ready to disgorge itself. To Jo's mortification, his blood goes crazy, half of it setting his ears alight and the rest plummeting to make his trousers twitch. He keeps his eyes trained on the toes of his boots, just to avoid the barrage of new words that enter his mind at this woman's attire.

She doesn't seem to notice his discomfort and continues condescendingly with a sweeping gesture at the frescoes. "The glories of the Haldrian Empire are the pride of this city. We are famed for our artistic representation of great events."

"Oh, yes," Jo mumbles, his attention still fixed on his boots.

She sighs, exasperation oozing. "During the Cahaya festival, this floor becomes a pictorial representation of all in the empire that is worth noting. At noon on those days, this haphazard play of light becomes a coherent display of colour and artistic skill. It is something to behold. Alas, you have missed the festival by a few weeks."

He grunts this time, and she turns her gaze back to him. Jo feels the ice in her stare and suppresses a shiver. "You know, I invited her ladyship to attend your debut today, but she dismissed the matter entirely, even though I'm the imperial ambassador to Téarman. How does it feel to be renounced by your beloved *Master*?"

Jo looks up. The nastiness in her tone riles him. He wants to defend Viola from this horrible individual, but he knows it could put her in very real danger—especially if she manages to escape, as his vision from the Mother-Father indicated she might. Instead, he meets the ambassador's gaze as coolly as he dares and shrugs. "What her imperial highness chooses to do is none of my business. I only know that I studied under the greatest storyteller to grace this empire, and for that, I am grateful."

The woman's face turns stony, and he realises he has

touched a nerve. He hit the mark, for he wasn't sure if Viola was imperial royalty—possibly a princess. From the woman's reaction, he deduces the truth. *No wonder they've been trying to get her back. Even if it's just to make a point. From what I've heard, the hierarchy is very rigid.*

Jo notices her eyes shift from cold indifference to steely determination. "You should stay in Baile, even if it is only for a few days."

He also realises that the people here on Téarman, this key planet of the empire, stand to lose a lot if Viola disappears. *I hope she succeeded*, he thinks. Out loud, he says, "I thank you for the offer, Milady, but I am forced to decline. When one studies an art, such as mine, it is important constantly to be studying and practising. I fear I have already lost valuable time by staying as long as this. I should get to Abhainn as soon as I can. It is not far, is it, Milady?"

"Well, since you insist. I will have everything readied, and you may leave once the afternoon's rain passes. If you leave on a fast hovercraft this afternoon, you can get there by mid-morning tomorrow."

Jo nods. "Thank you, Milady. I must go and fetch my belongings."

"Yes, of course. Although you need not go yourself. We will have your things fetched for you. There is no point risking a drenching in the coming downpour."

Chapter Twenty-Two

Viola trudges into a twilight of verdant woods through which the road cuts like a beige scar. The air is muggy, and she watches tendrils of steam curling from the hot surface of the road that still glistens from the storm.

Stillness envelops her. The only sounds she makes out are her breathing and the squelches her sodden shoes give off with every step. *Why are there no animal sounds?* A shiver runs through her, and she glances up into the trees, but they're deserted. The canvas of green isn't even painted with colourful flowers. Occasional brown stems and grey bark are the only breaks in the monotony.

No buzzing insects flit about. The skies are empty of birds. *When I last came through here, it abounded with life.* Green sentinels stand around her—stern and silent—and the lack of animation seeps into her core, sapping her life-giving warmth. She recalls that there was no sound of animals in the ambassador's garden, either. Her awareness latches onto the dampness of her clothes. She increases her pace in the hope that in the late afternoon heat she'll warm her body and the clothes will dry.

The silence is broken by a gentle hum that grows ever louder. Viola turns in the direction of the sound and makes out a sleek object hurtling up behind her. She hastens to the side of the road, her heart hammering in her ears. *The boy's distraction cannot have been long-lived. Chances are, they have already discovered that I am missing; this could be the frontline of their search.*

On the verge of diving into the undergrowth to hide, Viola calms herself. She's in disguise and should rather not draw any attention. *Head down and keep going. I am a traveller going to Coill.*

She feels the cold in earnest now and wonders how she's going to survive this ordeal. Her feet are icy despite the warmth of the afternoon. A blast of wind buffets her as the hovercraft zooms past. She glances up and meets familiar wide brown eyes. Goosebumps break out on her arms, and not just in response to the vehicle's slipstream. *There are no coincidences.*

The hum from the hovercraft grows louder as it banks and returns. Viola steps back, and it pulls up beside her to reveal her apprentice who grins at her from the back seat, mischief glinting in his eyes.

"Good afternoon," he says, his voice feigning ignorance of her identity while his eyes sparkle with that secret knowledge.

Viola responds with a soft, "G'day." She nods at him and the two burly men seated in the front of the craft.

"I've had the good fortune of receiving a ride to Abhainn," says Jo. "Would you care to join me, traveller?" When she nods and steps towards the craft, he adds, "For as far as your journey takes you along this road, of course."

She smiles, briefly meeting the gaze of the two men sitting in the front of the craft. The one closest to her wears his hair in a topknot, strands swept from their confines by the wind. His eyes are hard, and irritability rolls in palpable waves off both him and the driver. Hurrying, Viola steps up onto the craft, putting on a local accent, "Why, thank ye. Y'er very kind."

She settles into the seat beside Jo and sees to it that her illusion holds in place. Then, mentioning another town on the road to Abhainn, she adds, "I'm a'headin' to Coill."

With a whirr of the engine, the open transport shoots forward, bombarding them with cold air. Viola bites down on her lower lip to stop her teeth from chattering, while Jo launches into the story of his life—or, at least, an entertaining version of certain parts of it. One guard sighs while the other looks back and rolls his eyes. Her apprentice is doing this for their benefit. *They only see an airhead boy—what fools.* No light emanates from him during his monologue. *He is doing a good job of keeping his magic under wraps.*

She joins in the ruse by asking pertinent questions and pretending to be an avid listener. All the while, she discreetly observes the guards. The man in the passenger seat keeps glancing at her, unsettling Viola's already frazzled nerves. Some time later, the vehicle comes to an abrupt halt. Viola is flung forward, a cry escaping her lips.

"Coill is down that road," the driver grunts, nodding off to the right with his head.

Viola comes to her feet with a groan. Her toes are lumps of ice, and her fingers ache from the cold of being in damp clothes. Her whole body is stiff. Jerkily, she manages to climb out of the transport and step onto the road without falling over.

"Thank ye, kind sirs, that was quick," she says, bowing her head slightly to Jo and glancing at the two guards in the front.

She begins to walk up the side road, then stops. *I do not remember this place.* Her heart starts beating faster. *I have been tricked.*

In the same instant, the guard in the passenger seat says, "Well, well, well. You're clearly not who you say you are. Anyone from these parts would know this isn't the road to Coill. How is your seat wet when your clothes are dry? Who are you? And what were you doing in Baile?"

The man climbs out of the vehicle in a fluid motion. Viola sees a baton in his hand and begins to tremble. She knows she can't outrun him, but she can't stand and fight either. She has no weapon, and even with one, she is lethargic, frozen to the bone.

Jo pops his head over the side and hollers, "Catch!" while tossing her compacted bamboo staff to her. Viola grabs the whirling object on instinct alone. Her frozen hands fumble with it for a moment, and then she pulls it out to its full length while thanking her intuitive gesture of gifting him her backpack.

The other guard now climbs out of the hovercraft and both advance on Viola, their truncheons swinging in their hands. Viola glances over at Jo, hoping he's remembered that there's more to her staff than this.

He's been waiting for her. She watches his arm arc and then a pink object pelts the ground at her feet, sparking a shower of sand onto her legs. Viola scoops up the quartz crystal and affixes it to the top of the bamboo rod.

Her attackers pause their advance, and an uncertain glance passes between them. The one with the topknot spits and growls, "So you *are* a witch! You do know the penalty for anyone who uses magic outside of the imperial family and the Tower of Mages?"

From her peripheral vision, Viola sees Jo slip into the front seat of the vehicle. Keeping her eyes on the guardsmen, she tries to gauge what to do. To buy some time, she smiles, intimating some secret knowledge.

"What?" the other guard voices his confusion. Viola only deepens her smile in answer.

Then Jo pokes his head out above the door. He lifts both his thumbs in front of his face and grins at her. She's planned her next move and raises the staff swiftly, bringing it down to the ground with a crackling flash. Then she's sitting beside Jo who presses the accelerator, and they screech forward, billowing dust behind them, leaving the two guards coughing and choking.

"Did you see their faces?" Jo crows with glee.

Viola chuckles at his exuberance, then says, "Let me drive. From the sound of the engine, you do not have the first idea of how to keep this thing functional."

"Awww. But it's so much fun!" he whines, although he takes his foot off the accelerator.

The machine begins to slow, then spins unexpectedly out of control.

"What the—?" Jo exclaims.

The hovercraft makes an about-turn and hurtles ever faster back the way they came.

"Jump!" Viola shouts, flinging herself from the craft. She rolls, shielding her compacted staff, and comes to her feet, cursing the ache in her knee that has intensified after her stint in the rain. Jo tumbles out a moment later, and they watch the vehicle speed away down the road.

"What just happened?" he gasps out between breaths.

"They must have a remote-control device and called it back. They will be through here any minute now. We need to vanish. Quick!"

They push into the undergrowth on the side of the road. Once they're out of sight, Viola taps her stave to the ground. A rustle spreads out, and their footprints disappear, along with all other signs of their passing.

"Not a moment too soon," she mutters as they hear the approaching hum of the vehicle.

The two guards speed by and Viola takes note of Jo's sigh of relief. "It is not over yet, boy. We cannot walk through the undergrowth; they will be back and forth this way for a while yet, and they will be able to hear and even see our movements. It is light enough and—strangely—there is no other noise in this forest." She pauses. "I do not understand what has happened to the wildlife that should be here."

"It is spooky," he breathes.

They sit in stillness, hardly daring to breathe, and listening to the quiet around them. Viola's clothes are still damp, but she's relieved at how much her limbs have warmed since she started moving. She's now on the verge of breaking out into a sweat. After a few minutes, the threatening sound of the hovercraft thrums around them. It fills Viola's mind, grating on her nerves. Moments pass before the silver machine comes into view, crawling down the road as the two men search for signs of footprints.

She holds her breath, pressing herself against a tree trunk, as they inch past. The barrage of her heart is so loud that Viola could swear the guards will hear it, but they pass by without stopping. When the vibration of the engine fades into nothingness, Jo straightens and wipes his hands on his trousers.

"I'm sorry; we lost your pack," he says, a rueful smile on his lips.

"We have what's most important." Viola gestures to the staff in her hand. "Thank you, Jo. You did really well. How did all of this come about? I did not think I would get to see you again—and your note was so cryptic."

He grins. "I had a dream. I saw myself standing before a great crowd of people, telling *The Companion's Tale,* and somehow, I knew doing so would allow you to escape. In the dream, I saw the backpack, so I knew I needed to take it with me. I—" He trails off, excitement dissolving from his face. His head tilts to one side and Viola makes out the renewed sound of the hovercraft's engine.

"Here we go again," she murmurs.

They crouch down and wait. Time slows. Viola is once more subsumed into the beating of her heart as the fear of discovery pounds through her. Something brushes her arm, and she jumps, stuffing her fist against her teeth to stop from crying out.

"Everything is going to work out," Jo whispers. "They haven't found us yet, and that means there's hope we can stay hidden."

Her throat constricts, and she nods.

The stillness returns and Jo is on his feet in a matter of moments. "With your magic, can you dampen the sound of our passing?"

Viola blinks, not understanding.

"If you can muffle the sound of us walking, then we can move. When we hear them coming back, we stop for a rest. Eventually, we'll get beyond the section they're searching, and we'll be free. Would that be possible?"

Viola hisses air through her teeth. "Yes, it can be done. I should have thought of it myself. I do not know why my mind seems so addled today."

He smiles, grabs her elbow and begins walking. They stay a few paces from the road, and keep going, stopping only when the sound of the hovercraft indicates their pursuers are near. The afternoon slides into evening. A cool breeze rustles through the vegetation and the shadows of the forest deepen.

"We're going to spend a night in the creepy forest," Jo clasps his hands together and grins; his teeth are bright ivory in the shadowy forest.

Viola's nerves fray. *He sounds far too happy at the prospect,* she thinks, wrinkling her face. She doesn't say anything, though. Their pursuers pass again, and Viola clings to the hope that this will be the guards' last pass before they give up. Then she hears something else, and her heart almost stops.

Chapter Twenty-Three

The forest is quiet. Only the breeze rustles through the canopy above. Darkness has descended although Jo can still make out the barren swath of the road in the half-light beyond the trees. He picks out the sound of baying dogs. Lights dance in the distance, and he can make out voices. The hum of engines increases and he realises there are many hovercraft about now.

"They have joined up with the search party looking for me," Viola whispers.

"Dogs are a problem," Jo whispers back.

"Yes! Yes, they are."

Something filters into his mind. It is a soft tinkle—far distant. "There's a stream!" He quivers with excitement. "If we can find our way to it, we can use it to lose the dogs."

"I cannot hear anything," Viola whispers. "Are you sure?"

"Yes."

He takes her hand and leads her through the darkening wood while she does her best to mask their passing.

Soon, the tension in Viola releases as her shoulders relax, and her gait becomes less agitated. "I can hear it too."

He nods, and they keep going. It is almost completely dark when they come to a trickling waterfall that spills into a sluggish stream. Debris and sickly yellow scum float on the surface. The water glows phosphorescent and Jo's nose wrinkles under the assault of rot.

He pauses. Some presence beyond his grasp or understanding tugs at his senses. It is huge. Powerful. "I think we should—" His words are cut off by a soft splash as Viola steps into the stream.

A ripple of energy pulsates through the ground, and Jo's uneasiness increases. With his intestines roiling, he dashes forward, grabbing Viola. She swears, but he pulls with all his might. "Get out of there, now!" he screams.

Bewildered, her eyes wide, she follows him away from the water. A crash reverberates through the forest. The creaking, tearing sound of splintering wood reaches his ears and Jo runs, hoping Viola will also choose self-preservation. He dashes through the dark undergrowth, dodging trees while the sounds of destruction come ever closer. Another ripping crack tears through the air as a tree goes down, thundering as it flattens the underbrush and sending a tremor through the forest floor. Jo's toe catches on a twisted root, and he hurtles headlong into the dirt, his jaw slamming on the ground.

As he tries to get up, Viola comes careening into view and trips over his foot, tumbling down beside him. The crashing destruction of trees from one side and the barking of dogs from the other close in on them.

Jo tries once more to come to his feet, but pain shoots up from his left ankle. A cry rips out of him, and he collapses back onto the ground. Tears sting in his eyes and he brushes them away as his foot continues to throb, a dull cousin to the searing edge of a moment before.

Viola is on her feet again; Jo watches her turn towards him as a ghastly roar tears through the forest. He cowers and hears the barking behind them turn into terrified whines. Voices shout out in fear, and as Jo watches, a gargantuan shadow whips like a dancer's silken scarf across the undergrowth and past the place where he lies, unimaginable weight leaving a path of devastation behind it. The creature throws itself off the ground, head weaving, and trees shudder under its weight, branches cracking and leaves raining onto the loam below. Undulating scales seem to absorb the ambient light, but although they darken the night further, they remain blacker still. A word flashes through Jo's mind, and he almost laughs at the absurdity that he knows what will kill him but cannot stop it, because the word means nothing to him.

This is it, he thinks, but the monster gives another ear-splitting roar and snakes back towards the panicked movement of those in pursuit.

"What was that?" Viola's voice trembles.

"Does *Leviathan* mean anything to you?"

A strangled squeak escapes her.

Further screams erupt, ripping apart the forest's tranquillity, but Jo hears Viola's shallow breathing above it all. She begins muttering to herself, and her words draw his thoughts away from the pain in his ankle and the sounds of terror around him.

"We are all dead," she says. "No one can make it. I am going to be dinner for a mythical monster."

He sits up and grimaces, but focuses on Viola's panic instead of his discomfort. "Master," he says, willing his voice to be calm. "Earlier, you created a portal and transported yourself into the seat of the vehicle." He pauses, waiting for her to give a sign that she's listening. Her muttering stops, so he continues. "Do it now. Get back to the road, even if you have to do that trick from tree to tree. Find a transport and be on your way."

"I am not leaving you here, boy!" she exclaims, her

voice gruff. “Why do you insinuate that I would save my own skin? Do you think I have no honour?”

Jo shakes his head. “I can’t walk,” he whispers. “My ankle is hurt.”

The quartz on her staff comes alive. Jo blinks a few times, his eyes struggling to adjust to the change. He catches a glimpse of her crouching two strides from him, the staff in her right hand, the left shielding her eyes to adjust faster to the brightness. “Ah, there you are,” she says before plunging them back into the dark.

The inky blackness seems thicker than it was before she turned on the light. Jo shivers and tries to think of anything other than the sickening crunches and blood-curdling shrieks that fill the forest.

He feels Viola’s fingers dig into his armpit. “Get up!” she groans as she hoists him upright. “Lean on me. I think I still have enough strength to get us both out of here.”

“Oh,” he gasps as pain shoots to his knee. “I thought you could only transport yourself.”

She doesn’t answer. A tingling sensation prickles the hairs on his arms into static, and suddenly they’re beyond the treeline, but they can still hear the horrifying sounds of death emanating from the forest behind them. Viola sags against him, and Jo realises she’s used up too much energy transporting both of them this far.

He glances about as he tries to support her without

putting any weight on his injured foot. A short distance from them, a series of dark shadows are scattered about. He points and Viola nods. The prickling on his arms starts again and then they're sitting in one of the transports.

Viola droops in the seat, but still, she gets the machine under her control in a matter of moments, and they set off through the darkness. Once they're well enough away from the discernible sounds of carnage, she stops the craft. "Rest," is all she says before slumping against the seat.

His heart pounding loudly, Jo reaches over. She's cold, and her pulse is shallow. He searches around the vehicle, but there's no blanket or anything else he can use to cover her and keep her warm. With worry corroding his insides, Jo sits and waits, checking on Viola's pulse every so often and listening into the darkness, straining for any sounds.

Time converges on the moment, trapping him in its coils, just like it froze the meerkats a few months ago. Although the forest is still, Jo's mind fills it with his memory of the horrors that transpired in Téarman's rainforest. He reconstructs the sounds of death in all their gory details, lamenting his inaction. *I should have done something. There was so much death, and I did nothing more than save myself.*

Then another thought counters his rebuke. *I was*

terrified and gave way to my fear. I'm still young; the Mother-Father can forgive me if I learn my lesson here today. He sits up straighter in the seat, and the memories of crunching bones and screams cut off mid-cry fade into the rustling of the leaves. The gentle air caresses him—a sign of encouragement and a blessing. *Wind. Breath. Life.*

Do what you can today to make tomorrow better. The ordinance rings in his mind.

What can I do?

He thinks for a while, drifting on the edge of sleep. His memories wander further afield to a day when he faced death on his distant home planet. He recalls the horde of meerkats with their bared fangs. *I was afraid then, too.* His plea for it all to stop strikes a gong deep in his inner self. *I did that. I stopped them. If I could stop death there, then I can also stop it here.*

The serpent in the forest fills his thoughts once more. Its speed and size remind him of diverging realities. *The meerkats may have been many, but they were small. This gigantic creature, this Leviathan, was old and even magical. It would take more than my will to subdue such a thing and return it to its natural state.* He knew this was beyond his abilities, for now.

What can I do?

The answer is resounding when it comes. *Learn!* thinks Jo. He nods to himself. He needs to learn everything he can and improve his skills. He's only beginning to understand what he's capable of and decides it will be best, for the moment, to follow Viola's advice and train with the musician, since she pointed out that structure is as important as the words themselves.

His body relaxes with the knowledge. He'll become a magic-user in his own right, using the conjuring that comes with words. Once he's stronger and has more control, he's determined to face the Leviathan. After that, he will go back to Mshrali, where he can stop more children from dying and more towns from being abandoned. *I'll save all the other creatures from the blight, just like those meerkats. This is my purpose. I know what I must do.*

His breathing deepens, and within moments, he slips into the calm of deep sleep.

Chapter Twenty-Four

Viola wakes with a start. She sits up, the miasma of sleep still tugging at her consciousness. Bleary-eyed, she looks about, taking in the transport she's sitting in, her apprentice snoring softly beside her. The deep shadows of the forest whisper in a breeze. Far distant in the midnight canopy, she can make out a few silver stars dotting the sky.

Having found her bearings, she takes stock of herself. Her body aches all over, and icy fingers have a hold of her bones. Her mind is filled with the memory of a slithering, coiling shadow speeding through the forest, sending countless trunks splintering to the ground and filling the air with cries of horror. *Flitting like that with the boy was quite reckless of me*, she thinks. *Well, it was do or die; I could not leave him there, injured or not. And we are safe—for now.*

She starts up the engine and peers into the gloom ahead of her. Then she checks the dashboard, sensing buttons by touch. "Damnation!" she exclaims. *I need light!*

Her arm brushes against the object in her lap. She grasps her staff and sighs, calling forth a glow. It doesn't take her long to find the button she's searching for.

A blaze sears through the darkness, blotting out the shadows ahead of her transport. Viola shields her eyes from the glare until they've adjusted. Her cheeks crease into a smile, and as she plays her fingers over the dashboard, the machine hums into motion. The craft hurtles through the air, driving a chill wind through her. Viola slows the hovercraft and turns her attention back to the buttons in front of her. After a search, she gives one a light touch and a transparent shell snaps into place above the cab.

"That is much better," she murmurs as they hurtle through the night.

When dawn begins to brighten the tops of the trees, Viola floats the craft in among the trunks and out of sight of the road. She clambers out and pulls branches and twigs into place around the transport, obscuring it from view. Then she slips inside once more and settles back to sleep.

When she wakes, it's the natural floating back to consciousness that comes after a deep and restful sleep. Her eyelids flutter a few times and then, pushing herself up, she stretches her arms. The boy shifts in the seat beside her and she watches him look about, bewilderment evident in his large brown eyes.

"I woke in the night and drove as far as I dared before hiding us here. We do not want to be about during daylight hours. The empire will not let a few deaths stop their hunt for me if they know I am alive. We have to hope they believe everybody died last night."

He nods, shifting his body, then winces. She sees him glance at his feet and remembers his injury. "Let me take a look at that foot of yours," she adds.

The boy grimaces as he lifts his leg towards her outstretched hands. The ankle is swollen, and he suppresses a cry when she pulls his boot free to reveal mauve transitioning through violet over his foot and lower leg.

Her long years travelling brought with them a fair share of injuries, but she sighs, worry creasing her brow. "I don't think I can heal this. I have used too much magic in the last day for it to be safe. You are going to have to avoid walking for the foreseeable future, and I shall do what I can to ease the pain while it heals."

"Do you think it's broken?" his voice is low and she hears the fear trembling there.

"I cannot say for certain. I do not want to hurt you to find out. With a little more rest, I may be able to probe it magically and get a better idea."

Jo nods and returns his leg to his side. "Good thing we have this transport," he manages to grin, "because as you say, I'm not going to be walking anywhere for the next while."

Viola pats his shoulder companionably. Then she glances out into the forest. It is as quiet as it was when they first entered it, and the sun streams through the thick canopy, speckling the ground with light.

"We also need food," she mutters.

She turns and runs her hands over the seat behind them. "Ah, there it is!" she exclaims. In the next instant, the seat springs open, revealing a compartment underneath. She pulls out a blanket and several packs of travel food.

They eat in a silence broken only by the rustling of wrappers and the sound of chewing. The boy licks his fingers and then glances at the torn casings littering the craft.

"Why do people here create so much waste?"

Viola shrugs. "I suppose it is the price of civilisation."

His look turns sullen. "That doesn't go with what I've

learned. We are intelligent beings created as custodians by the Mother-Father. It isn't natural that we should destroy everything we've been tasked with protecting."

"You see, that is your problem," she replies, shaking her head, and with a loud rustle, gathering up the wrappings. "You believe the best of humanity. But humanity does terrible things. We kill indiscriminately. We are greedy and do everything to accumulate wealth while keeping others from sharing in it. There is nothing good about us. Just think about it; humans are pretty much the only intelligent creatures left in all the empire—possibly the universe. We have marginalised, killed, and driven to extinction all the other beings such as elves, kobolds, and trolls.

"Humans dominate every planet in this empire, and they are destroying the natural habitats of all the other creatures on those planets too. We are a great disease, multiplying and destroying wherever we go. Where is your *Great Parent* in all of that? What parent would allow for some of their children to destroy all the others? Perhaps we are more like a virus, meant to destroy planets to keep some sort of greater balance." She catches sight of him shaking his head and adds, "Come on! Humans commit horrifying atrocities at every turn. You could not know that because you have not experienced much from your sheltered life in Fásach."

"That's why we have choice," he whispers.

Viola feels her exasperation mounting, a towering wave ready to crush all that lies beneath it.

He raises a hand and clarifies, his voice becoming stronger with each word. "A parent can't stop a child from making mistakes or injuring themselves. I took care of a lamb once. Shefele's mother died, so I got to raise her. I wanted to protect her all the time, to keep her from any dangers, but the more I did that, the more Shefele bleated and struggled to be free. When I let her go, she learned from the other sheep and followed their lead. I think we learn by example, which is why there's an ordinance from the Great Parent to *be the change you want to see*."

"I suppose you may be right. I can imagine, if I had a child, I would have to let them make their own mistakes and rather than guarding them against harm, it would be better to teach them to be self-sufficient in moments of adversity. Yes, you make a good point." She pauses, thinking on his words, then adds, "Come to think of it, that is exactly what my mother did wrong. She tried to rule my life and commanded me on how to live. That made me do the exact opposite of what she wanted. I refused her out of wilfulness and spite." She chuckles. "And yes, being an example is probably the best way forward, although it is very hard in this world of greed and egoism. How do you find the right path when all those around you behave like a scourge on the universe?"

Glancing at Jo, she sees the flash in his eyes. His mouth opens, but she cuts him off, "Yes, yes. I know. *Choice*. Free will is everything."

"And intuition," he adds. His lips twitch heavenward, but that small smile brings an ache to her heart.

Rain begins falling, drowning out their conversation with a thundering patter on their hovercraft. They wile away the afternoon, drifting between sleep and wakefulness until the storm passes and leaves the world outside dripping. As the shadows lengthen in response to the setting sun, Viola rouses herself and prepares to guide the craft from the underbrush.

That night in the comfort of the hovercraft, they travel far through the tropical wilderness. At intervals they pass towns—at that late hour, they're dark shadows nestled in large clearings. Viola dims the headlights when passing those and they move along unnoticed. She enjoys listening to Jo as he recounts tales for her. She marvels at how quickly he learned the craft. *He is a natural*, she thinks as he weaves a tapestry out of words.

Dawn comes. They're hidden among the leaves as the rays of first light spill into their daytime retreat. The golden sun spears its shafts through the canopy, highlighting varying shades of green. Viola gives thanks for this boy who insisted that she be his teacher and he her student. Pride swells in her heart, warming her from the inside out. The sensation is mirrored outside by the life-giving warmth the heavenly orb sends out to all things that its luminous fingers caress.

She falls asleep with a smile on her lips and gratitude in her heart.

Chapter Twenty-Five

Jo wakes with a start at the harsh sound of rainwater pelting the surface just above his head. He stretches and glances over at Viola who groans and pushes herself into a sitting position. Her lips are cracked with dry ravines, and he notices his own thirst. Turning to the open seat behind him, Jo rummages until he finds the last bottle of water they have.

He passes the flask first to Viola. Her eyes twinkle her thanks, and she tips the liquid down her throat. When she's done, she hands it back to him. "Did you sleep well?"

He nods, wiping excess water from his lips.

"There is some time before we can head out safely. I have been wondering; just before I left the spaceship, we determined that turning myself in and going back to my family was the right thing to do. Why did you go back on that and let me escape?"

Jo searches for a way to explain. "I had this feeling," he says tentatively. "The situation didn't sit right with me. I felt there was a better way. What I mean is, I sensed you were meant to go back on your own terms, not at their whim. And I had that dream, too."

Her gaze holds his. He senses appreciation and gratitude emanate from her when she says, "I am thankful you did. I couldn't bear all the posturing and manoeuvring they were doing because of this. I still do not quite understand why I wasn't taken directly into the legion's custody, but I suppose I should accept the blessings I have been given."

Joy blazes through him. "You're finally understanding," and he can't help the grin from spreading across his face.

Viola chuckles. "No need to get presumptuous."

He feels his face muscles pull wider and winks. "I knew it was just a test to see whether you were ready to choose a different path. I'm glad we could share this adventure. It hasn't been as scary as it could have been, just because you're here with me."

"You know I shall not be able to stay when we get to Abhainn." Her voice turns serious.

"I know," says Jo. "I have my path to take, my purpose to fulfil, and so do you. After seeing the Leviathan, I understand better what it is I must do. I have to learn and improve my skills, and you said Cerddor will help me with that. Your path will take you where it must; hopefully, one day, our roads will be allowed to cross again."

There's sadness in Viola's eyes, so Jo leans forward and pats her arm. "That is life. It has always been that way. We can accept it and find our path, our meaning."

She sits in silence, her thoughts taking her far away. At length, she muses, "What is the meaning of life? It seems so pointless sometimes."

"What is the meaning you assign to your life, Master? What do you do, what actions do you take, to uphold that meaning and express it?"

Stillness spans for an eternity between them. Comfortable. Companionable. Then she shifts. Light blazes through her being, gleaming from her violet eyes with an enlightened twinkle. "I am here," Viola says, determined. "I exist, and I am alive. That is something to be grateful for." She pauses. Jo watches her gathering her thoughts, taking the next step.

"What am I actually doing?" she asks, turning inward. "What is the point of being alive if I cannot be me?"

Jo feels sparks of excitement coursing through him. This is a moment he's longed for, and it thrills him to be present at such a convergence.

Viola continues, "My storytelling barely scratches the surface of what I am capable of achieving. I know what I must do, although I do not know how I shall achieve it. Still, it is the time to act. I need to take responsibility. I have spent years avoiding my duty and running away from the truth I have known in my heart. If I am to move forward, I must take the reins back into my hands, and I understand how I shall do that. There is a person I need to meet."

Her mouth falls open when another thought strikes her. Jo shifts to the edge of his seat. "Who is it, Master? What are you thinking of?"

She lets out a soft gasp before answering. "Can it be a coincidence that the one person I have to see—now—should be here on Téarman?"

"Ah, Master. You should know by now. *There are no coincidences*, only a carefully laid out plan that we muddle our way through because we're flawed human beings."

She nods her head. As she shifts in her seat, her surprise transforms into resolve. "Ready for the next leg of the journey?"

Jo inclines his head.

Late in the night, the stars myriad pinpricks in the sodalite canopy, Jo peers into the darkness beyond the vehicle's headlights. The hovercraft is slowing, and he looks about. Trees still rise into the sky on both sides of the sheer thoroughfare they're on. He glances at Viola, whose eyes are searching for something along the side of the road.

Then she swings her arms, turning and guiding the vehicle between some trees into the darkened growth of the rainforest. Branches scrape on the smooth surface of the transport, grating on Jo's ears and raising the hairs on his arms.

"Why are we stopping?"

"Abhainn is close. We shall be there in about two hours of walking. We would have been here days ago if we had managed to hop into the extra-fast hovercraft you and those guards were in. But the journey was pleasant enough, even though we did not get to see much of the beauty of this land and its towns." She shrugs. "Ah, well, our destination is near and now it is time we leave this craft behind."

He glances at his foot, still tender from the fall a few days before, and then looks at her again. "I thought I wasn't supposed to walk."

She gestures for him to give her his foot, and she prods it.

Jo bites on his lip in preparation for the pain, but when it doesn't come, he takes a closer look. Warmth tingles through his ankle as her fingers whisper over his skin, then the sensation disappears. The bruise has faded and the discomfort subsided.

Viola gives a satisfied grunt and murmurs, "That should help speed up your natural healing. It will be good as new by morning. We are all set."

Sunlight wakes Jo. It streams onto his face and heats the enclosed capsule of the transport to an uncomfortable level. He rummages for a water bottle, but there's nothing. He swallows against his thirst and looks over to Viola. She hands him the bottle from the day before. There's one sip left, and he holds it in his parched mouth where it cools the ache of his thirst.

Viola presses the button to pop back the transparent cover and hops out, coming around to his side of the vehicle. He grabs the hand she extends to him and steps down, testing his injured foot.

"Let's go!" she calls, her voice bright.

As he walks out into the road, the air around Viola shimmers and her shape transforms. Her jaw broadens, and her eyes turn a muddy brown. Her clothes shift from tattered white to a copy of Jo's brown trousers and his tunic, cinched at the waist with a belt. Heavy brown boots hide her feet. Her staff turns into a simple walking stick.

"How'd you do that?" he asks.

"It is a simple trick of willing the air to express an

image held in my mind. It is an easy enough illusion if you figure out the basics of it."

He tries to copy the action he saw her make with her hands and a ripple flits around him, but nothing else happens.

"Come along. We do not have time for that."

He follows her up the road, whistling a tune.

After trudging for close to three hours, they reach a break in the treeline along the banks of a river. The brown churning waters stretch far into the distance, and he can only just make out a belt of dark green on the other side, separating the brown from the azure above.

His gaze is drawn off to one side, to a conglomeration of bright colours. There are fewer than ten houses there, but each one is a different colour. Through a wide opening in a pink building, which is nearest the piers, Jo makes out some benches.

"Well, here you are," Viola says with a sigh. He glances up at her. A nostalgic look settles in her gaze as she contemplates a purple building and nods towards it meaningfully. "This is where we part ways, boy."

Jo's mind races with a thousand thoughts. She puts her hand on his shoulder, and a lump grows in his throat until it becomes too painful to speak.

"For now, stay here and study under Cerddor. He is a good man and a miracle worker when it comes to music." She glances up at the amethyst cottage again, then shakes her head. "I cannot come with you. I doubt I would be welcome there and it is best you arrive only with my recommendation. Besides, I have those things I need to do." Her smile is sad when she adds, "I am very glad we met and even happier you convinced me to take you on as my apprentice. You have a bright future, Jo, my boy. Take care of yourself."

Movement catches Jo's eyes as a man with a heavy beard steps out of the pink building. Viola glances over to him and waves. He returns her greeting, and she gestures towards the pier, indicating that she's looking for a boat to take her across. The man calls her over.

Viola turns to Jo and pushes something cool into his hand. "Here is everything I know. I recorded all my tales while we were on the Startraveller's Hope. Cerddor should have a device so you can listen to them. I wish you all the best of luck, Jo."

Spinning on her heel, she strides towards the man who moves up onto the jetty. They disappear for a while and then bob back into view on a paddleboat. Jo watches the vessel bounce through the shallow waves of the river as paddles splash in a constant rhythm. Viola lifts her hand in a final farewell before turning her gaze to the opposite shore.

Jo stands on the riverbank and watches his teacher and friend become a tiny speck swallowed by the distance of swirling muddy waters.

. . .

My dear boy,

I have never been good at partings, and I hope you will forgive me. My life has not given me much opportunity to learn how to say farewell properly. I know you will expand your abilities under Cerddor's tutelage and I am certain you will do well there. This town is small, but everything in this empire is connected, so keep your head low and try to conceal your true skills. Cerddor may understand, but others are unlikely to see past a young man wielding power. Keep your focus on your studies, as I know you will, and all will be well.

There is someone I once knew, and I believe she lives in Bryniau; I realise I have some accounts to settle before I can truly achieve the goal I dream of. I shall do my best to return and see how you are doing once I have completed this task. Thank you for your patience and the insights you have given me. I know that at times I opposed you most harshly, but know that I do appreciate your thoughts and opinions.

Much must still be done, and I am aware of that more than ever. I have come to the realisation that I must return and speak with my family to resolve what has passed and to see whether we can come to some agreement that will be beneficial to them and me. I can see that little cottage in a quiet place with a dog warming itself by the fire. I look forward to a future working with stories but with the opportunity to stay in one place, and I hope, should our paths not meet before then, that you will find your way to my doorstep so we may converse again.

For now, learn what you can from Cerddor and combine what you learn here with what I have taught you. I believe the art of a bard will suit you greatly, and I am certain it will provide the opportunity for you to become a proper spellwright.

I bid you farewell and can only hope that your Great Parent will see to our meeting again. Farewell, apprentice.

A soft crackle is followed by silence. The boy falls back onto a quilt of many-coloured squares and stares up at the rough wooden ceiling. The silver device rests silent in his cupped hand. He gives thanks for the blessings of a fortuitous meeting and a great adventure. *Spellwright*, he muses with a smile. His mind drifts to the river whose rushing waters accompany him every moment of the day, and he dreams of a figure vanishing into the distance on her way to new adventures, a figure whom he might one day follow.

Epilogue

Monadir steps out of the cool speedcraft into the sweltering heat of Téarman. Thick air sticks to him, beading him in sweat. Brushing a hand over his neck, he stretches before looking at the cluster of people approaching him.

Their bright clothes sear his eyes. He shudders at the thought of wearing something in such a garish shade, rather than the familiar black and gold of the imperial military which he wears with pride. As if in response to his thought, his armpits decide to exude liquid, pointing out how inappropriate his military suit is in Téarman's incandescence.

The delegation pauses a few steps from him. A glance is exchanged between its members, hesitation oozing from them. The hairs on Monadir's arms prickle and his gut clenches. *What's happened now?*

A feminine figure detaches herself from the group. Her dark hair is pinned in an elaborate up-do, and her face is hidden under an inch-thick layer of paint. Her pink outfit with black polka dots makes her look like a watermelon. Monadir takes note of her movements. There's something familiar about the way she walks, the sway of her arms, the angle of her head, the way she leans forward to emphasise her ample bosom.

"Natesari, is that you?" he struggles to keep the disbelief from his voice.

"Ah, Monadir. It is a pleasure. How have you been? Where is my sense of hospitality? Come, join me for a cup of iced kekwa and we can catch up."

He shrugs and glances about. Urgency begins gnawing at him, the ever-present hound that is his determination. Shaking his head, he says, "I need to get the storyteller back to Empress Dedopali. The sooner, the better."

A shadow flits across Natesari's visage, and creases leave thin cracks in her copper makeup. "Um— Let us get inside, out of the heat, and I will tell you all about it."

"What happened?" The low rumble from his chest is threatening, and she takes two steps backwards.

"Um— Well— She escaped yesterday afternoon."

"*What?*"

"We sent an army out after her. Every city guardsman in Baile was ordered to bring her back." Her voice falters.

Horror laces it, etching more lines into the thick paste that obscures her features. "They are all gone. Vanished into the forest." Her pitch rises to a squeak, "No one returned."

Monadir's jaw locks. A conflagration tears through his veins and he knows Natesari sees it flare in his eyes because she takes two more faltering steps backwards.

"The last missive we received was a garbled message of screams and something about 'It is coming. Death is here'." A shudder runs through her. "No one brave enough is left. Baile is completely unprotected, and whatever happened will remain a mystery. The city gates will stay locked until the empress deigns to send us new recruits."

"Half-wits," Monadir growls. "I will do it myself."

He stalks off and the remaining Baileans part before him. Without a word, he strides past, Natesari hot on his heels, calling, "I will have a hovercraft ready right away. They were heading east. Her apprentice claimed he was going to Abhainn, but his escort never reported back either, so I do not know what happened."

Monadir grunts, drawing all his fury into a precise focus. He'll get that storyteller to the empress if it's the last thing he does. His hand wraps around the cool pendant hanging from his neck. The motion is so routine that he doesn't notice he has tugged it out from under his shirt. *Isperia, why do you keep slipping from my grasp?* He tucks the locket back in its place, out of sight, and focuses on the storyteller whom the empress ordered him to bring in.

A few hours later, Monadir pulls up beside a jumble of abandoned hovercrafts cluttering the middle of the road. His eyes scan the forest around him. No movement. No sound. The stillness is complete except for the gentle rustle of a breeze dancing among the leaves. Casting about on the edges of the road, he makes out some footprints and begins the painstaking task of following them into the half-light under the trees.

Sunlight streams into a clearing. Following the footprints, Monadir frowns at the unexpected brightness. He takes in the forest around him. A massive tree lies felled, allowing the light access to the ground where he stands. The lower part of the base remains, its roots anchored into the earth. The ten-foot trunk lies splintered beside it, crushing branches and leaves that have fallen from the surrounding trees.

He stares in bewilderment at the destruction. How could a tree that size be broken like that? It's an impossibility—but he is looking at it. Monadir shakes his head, trying to clear the blankness that threatens to overwhelm his senses.

An odour tingles in his nostrils. The sharp tang of iron tickles his senses. It is then that he notices the blood. Streaks of dried brown are everywhere; pools of blackened life-substance burn their way into his mind. Once he starts seeing things, he cannot unsee them: a tatter of red cloth hanging from a branch above, a black boot dangling from it; a handful of hair, still attached to a chunk of bloodied scalp; a dismembered hand, and guts spilling out from under the fallen tree trunk.

All the years of training are nothing. Monadir's stomach heaves. He turns away from the glade of death but only makes it a few steps before memory triggers the reflex in his stomach. Acid courses its way up his throat and he retches, the stench of bile lingering in his mouth and nose.

He repeatedly spits while walking back to his hovercraft. The silence of the forest is complete. He shudders at the thought of the sheer size of a creature capable of wreaking such destruction. Turning his mind to his assignment, he wonders whether the storyteller survived. His gut clenches—a different motion from before. This has nothing to do with the smell of death in the silent rainforest. His gut is telling him with absolute certainty that she is still alive. He recognises that feeling, the knowledge that resides deep within him. He has learned to trust in this intuition.

"No matter where you are, Viola Alerion, I will find you." Determination blazes within him. "I will succeed."

THE END

Join Viola and Jo as their journeys continue in:

Finding the Way
Becoming Spellwright
and
Master Wordmage

Want to stay up to date with the Wishmaster Series and the accompanying series of novellas, The Wordmage's Tales? Subscribe to my newsletter to get all pertinent updates about my new releases and get a free ebook of The Sewing Princess, one of the Wordmage's Tales. The Sewing Princess novella is available exclusively to my newsletter subscribers.

Acknowledgments

This book owes its existence to many amazing people. First, I would like to thank my mother, Anne, for fostering my love of words and encouraging me on my own journey to becoming a storyteller, and my father, Stephan, for always being so enthusiastic when it comes to history. I would not be who I am today without your constant care and all the fascinating tidbits of knowledge you both shared with me.

Danke, liebe Oma. Thank you, for showing me that we are never too old to do the things we are meant to do and for giving me the courage, by your example, to take life by the horns. Thank you for being my inspiration and my guiding light. I know you joined me on this journey—coming back from wherever it is your path has taken you—and helped me when I got stuck. You are sorely missed and deeply loved.

Tuomas Holopainen, thank you for your inspirational words that brought the spark of an idea into my life, halfway across the globe. And Tarja Turunen, thank you for your voice, which drew me out of my darkness and gave me glimpses of light. To the remaining band members of Nightwish, thank you for the music!

To those who contributed towards my crowdfund, thank you for making this dream a reality and for believing in Viola and me. Your support and engagement mean the world to me. Claire Stewart, Mahogany Silverrain, Caroline Bengtson, Astrid Provence, Alessandra Bosch, Samantha Graham, Douglas Pierce, Marie Hoping, Moira Floresta, Judith Korward, I cannot thank you enough! Extra special thanks go to Daphne Moore, Alice Gent and Amanda Marin. Thank you for believing in me and for raising me up and showing me what is possible. Of course, my family which has ever encouraged me, I thank you from the depths of my heart: Stella, Elena, Monika, Aliosha. Thank you for lightening the load and sharing your expertise to make this journey even more magical.

Special thanks go to my fabulous street team, Wishmaster's Book Angels: Samia, Yasmine, Lucy, Stefano, Matteo, Elena, Mariah, B.J. Facemire, Ann, Miriam, Mark, Kalisin, Silke, Missy Starkweather, Naomi, Sara, Jaime, Pheraday, Samantha Graham, Sherry, Oksana, Jo Harris, Dalila, Skye, Hannah, Marie, Tabitha, Milia,

Mariah, Julie, Patty, Samantha Seidel. Thank you for being my most loyal supporters. You are the best!

My amazing beta readers, Lena, Alice and Skye, thank you for your feedback and help. I am grateful for all the time you spent nurturing this seed so it could flourish and grow. Joy Sephton, my fabulous editor, thank you. You have been invaluable to this project. Emily, my cover designer, thank you for bringing Viola and her apprentice to life, visually. You are amazing and so incredibly talented.

I would also like to take this opportunity to thank the people who fostered my love of the English language and my desire to tell stories. Particular thanks go to Alan Northover, Mrs Van Loggerenberg, Mrs Erasmus and Mrs Bezuidenhoudt. Thank you for inspiring me and giving me the bedrock I needed to achieve my dreams.

Mary Morrissey, Jennifer Jimenez, Matt Boggs, John Boggs and Rich Boggs, thank you for leading the way and showing me what is possible. Jordan Peterson and Natalie Ledwell, I am grateful for all the work you do in inspiring others to make their lives better, and in doing so, helping me draw the veil from Viola's journey. This book required me to grow so much, and I couldn't have done it without your enlightenment.

To Julie Soper and Lawrence Switzer, I'd like to say: thank you for your words of encouragement and your enthusiasm. Your friendship means the world to me.

Julie, I honestly couldn't have done this without your constant support. You are the world's best accountability partner and the most amazing friend. You are a light in my life, and you've helped guide my way.

My husband, Renato, thank you for putting up with the awful hours, the long nights I have spent in the company of my computer instead of with you. Thank you for pushing me and making me keep my own deadlines, and thank you for just being there, always.

About the Author

Astrid Vogel de Johnsson is an award-winning South African author, social anthropologist and transformational life coach currently residing in Sweden. In early childhood, she showed an interest in reading and languages—interests which her family encouraged. Astrid started writing her first novel aged 12 and now writes fantasy in multiple sub-genres, exploring her passion for cultures, languages and the human capacity to achieve success in the face of overwhelming obstacles. She is fluent in 5 European languages, is happily married and has two adorable children. When she isn't writing, Astrid likes to read, take walks in nature, play silly games with her children, do embroidery and play music.

Also by Astrid V.J.

Elisabeth and Edvard's World

Gisela's Passion

Aspiring, Part 1 of the Siblings' Tale

Becoming, Part 2 of the Siblings' Tale

Naiya's Wish *

* Part of Enchanted Kingdoms Charity Box Set of Fairytales

Forthcoming

The Lion, the Lark and the Lady

Firmament

Down the Well

Johara's Choice

The Adventures of Tyrina Tursam

Pixie Tricks (A novella in the Ytherynia: Gifted Blood Academy Freshman anthology)

Blood Island

Spells and Potions (a novella in the Ytherynia: Gifted Blood Academy Sophomore anthology)

The Wishmaster Series

The Apprentice Storyteller, Book 1

Finding the Way, Book 1.5

Becoming Spellwright, Book 2

Master Wordmage, Book 3

The Wordmage's Tales

This is a series of novellas

The Companion's Tale

The Sewing Princess

The Artist and His Muse

The Last Warrior

Warring Lions

The Destitute Countess

Silvana's Trial

Dragons' Daughter

Divine Choice

The Showgirl

Made in the USA
Las Vegas, NV
18 June 2021

24958522R00184